MISDIAL

by

Rebecca Xibalba and Tim Greaves

(from an original idea by Rebecca Xibalba)

CHAPTER 1

It had been one of the warmest summers in Judy Harrison's memory.

There might have been a chill in the gentle south easterly sea breeze which caressed the streets of Eastbourne every morning to make it seem otherwise. But even Judy's – admittedly rose-tinted – childhood memories of holidays spent basking in unbroken sunshine had been eclipsed by this year's record temperatures. It had started unseasonably early at the beginning of May and even now, as the first day of September kissed farewell to a sultry August and the prospect of Autumn loomed, it was as hot as it had been in mid-July.

Judy opened her eyes and stared up at the white stuccoed bedroom ceiling above her. She'd been so deeply lost in a dream about her father that for a moment she wasn't actually sure where she was.

A movement in the bed beside her as her husband, Dave, stirred in his sleep and rolled over brought her mind sharply into focus. She turned her head and squinted at the bedside clock. The little red digits blinked at her: 06.02. No point even attempting to get back to sleep now, she thought. She'd have to be up in half an hour.

Not wishing to disturb Dave, she quietly turned her pillow and rested her head back down, savouring the feeling of the cool cotton on her neck. The scent of honeysuckle drifted in through the gently wafting curtains and each time they parted the sunlight flickered briefly across on her face. Her mind returned to the dream that was already beginning to fragment.

She'd been standing on a windswept beach assailed by little sand devils for as far as her eye could see. Within the skewed world of the dream she'd known exactly where she was; that deserted little stretch of coastline in France where Dave had taken her for their anniversary three years ago. But now, in the light of day, she realised it had born no resemblance to that at all.

Her father had been gone for almost two years and although she thought about him every day it had been a long time since he'd visited her dreams. She'd been urgently calling to him, yet no matter how loudly she cried out he seemed to be oblivious of her presence. She'd tried to run to him, but the distance between them just seemed to increase.

She suddenly felt an overwhelming urge to burst into tears. She put a hand to her mouth and drew on every ounce of the inner strength that had helped her so often since the day her father went into the ground at Bexhill Cemetery.

She looked at the clock again: 06:05. This is ridiculous, she thought, I may as well just get up.

She pulled back the duvet cover, swung out her legs and sat up on the edge of the bed. She glanced back at Dave. He was still sound asleep, making those little grunting noises she ribbed him about often and which he protested were a work of fiction on her part. She smiled and leaned over to plant a soft kiss on his forehead. Then she got out of bed and padded barefoot to the en-suite bathroom, slipping out of her chiffon nightgown as she went.

Getting out of bed and straight into the shower had always been up there among Judy's favourite moments of the day. It was a pleasure she never took for granted and as she luxuriated in the needles of warm spray peppering her skin, dousing the last remnants of her bad dream, her mind drifted to the day ahead. She must remember to call and book that table for Beryl's 70th.

Turning the temperature control, she stood for ten seconds as the warm water turned ice cold and afforded her the final wake-up-and-get-moving kick she always needed. Then she stepped out of the cubicle and briskly towelled herself dry. She looked at herself in the mirror. Still looking good at 42, she thought, and pulled a face.

With her wavy locks hanging wet around her shoulders – she detested hairdryers, always had – Judy crept back into the bedroom. She needn't have worried; Dave was still in the arms of Morpheus, the faint hint of a smile on his lips and that sporadic grunting louder now. She quietly dressed in her work clothes and went downstairs to the kitchen.

She was in the process of preparing herself a packed lunch when Dave, dressed only in his pyjama bottoms, stepped up behind her and slipped his arms around her waist.

"Oh!" she exclaimed. "I didn't hear you, you amorous devil."

She turned round and planted a kiss on his lips.

"Did I wake you?"

Dave stifled a yawn. "No, I was already awake."

Judy smiled at him. "You weren't, you know. You were soundo. And having yourself a nice little dream as far as I could tell."

Dave wiggled his eyebrows at her. "Oops. Was I playing tents?"

Judy's eyes widened and her mouth dropped open. "No!" She punched him playfully on the shoulder. "You were just grunting away rather contentedly."

"I do *not* grunt!"

Judy rolled her eyes. "Whatever. I was going to treat you to a cuppa in bed."

Dave's eyes lit up.

"But now you're here, how about you make me one instead?"

"Of course, m'lady." Dave chuckled.

While Judy finished readying her lunch, Dave prepared a hot drink for the two of them and they sat down at the kitchen table.

"What time's the film tonight?"

Dave looked thoughtful. "Er. I'm not sure. 6.30 I think. I'll check."

"It's Tuesday, so Beryl's giving me a lift home. I should be in by 5.30."

Dave took a sip of his tea. "That's cool. I was thinking we might grab something to eat afterwards if you fancy it. Chinese maybe?"

"Mmmm, sounds lovely."

*

Half an hour later, Judy was standing at the bus stop. There was really no need for her to be headed in on a 7.35, but as manager of the St Joshua's Hospice Charity Shop in town she always prided herself on being in an hour before opening.

As usual she was the only one waiting at the bus stop and it occurred to her, not for the first time, that it couldn't possibly be economical for the company to run a bus on this route – not at this time of the morning anyway. Most of the residents in the area were retired and probably weren't even out of bed yet. Those who might want to go in to town for that bit of shopping or to meet a friend for coffee wouldn't need the bus until mid-morning.

Judy pulled a paperback novel from her shoulder bag and removed the supermarket receipt she used as a bookmark. She'd never been a devout reader, but she enjoyed Anthony Horowitz's twisty-turny little thrillers; this one, 'The Word is Murder', was a particularly fiendish one and she grabbed every opportunity, no matter how fleeting, to read a bit more.

She'd barely got through a page before the bus appeared around the corner. She hastily tucked the receipt back in to mark her place, dropped the book back into her bag and raised a hand to catch the driver's eye. Never assume that the driver will stop for you just because you were waiting at the bus stop. That was something she'd learned the hard way.

CHAPTER 2

It had been a slow day overall, but with the last customer they'd be likely to see before closing time having spent more than enough to take them over the day's target, the mood in the St Joshua's Hospice Charity shop was buoyant.

The radio was on and Beryl Foster, whose 21-hour week ranked her as the closest to a full time volunteer the shop had, was standing at one of the display shelves dusting off china ornaments. As she carefully picked up each piece and flicked at it with her feather duster, she sang happily along to the song on the radio. As was usual for Beryl she didn't know half the words – even of the songs she liked – but that had never worried her.

Carrying a box of DVDs, Judy appeared from the back room. "Oi," she said sternly. "You're supposed to be working, not enjoying yourself."

Beryl stopped singing and looked up. She was fairly sure Judy was joking, but she could never be a hundred percent. She caught sight of the faint trace of a smile on her colleague's face.

"Well, not too much anyway." Judy set down the box of discs on the counter.

Beryl tutted. "I don't know when these shelves were last dusted, but this one's got at least two inches of accumulated gunk on it. Including several dead flies. You're lucky to have me and my faithful feather duster working for you."

"Well you'd better stop your moaning and get on with it."

Beryl waved the duster vigorously at Judy. "Cheeky sod!" One of the feathers came loose from the duster and Judy watched as it floated up and then made a perfect landing on Beryl's head. The two women burst out laughing.

"And hurry it up," Judy said, spluttering with laughter. "We'll be closing in half an hour."

Beryl fished the feather out of her hair and glanced at her watch. "Good Lord. Doesn't the time fly when you're having fun?"

"Sarcasm really doesn't suit you. Oh, by the way, are you still okay to run me home tonight? I'm only asking because…" She trailed off as she noticed Beryl's expression change.

"Oh crumbs, it's Tuesday, isn't it? I'm so sorry love; I've got to get the bus home."

"Oh no. Not car problems again?"

Beryl sighed. "Yes. I had to take the old girl to the garage on the way in this morning. Flipping clutch is playing up – again. I've got to call them tomorrow morning to get the verdict. I'm expecting bad news. Well, expensive news anyway. Sorry. I should have said earlier, but I completely forgot it's Tuesday."

Judy smiled. "Not a problem. I'll ring Dave. And don't worry about the bus – I'm sure we'll be able to drop you home."

She disappeared into the back room and reappeared a moment later clutching her mobile phone.

Beryl, who'd resumed her dusting regime, apologised again.

Judy smiled. "Honestly, don't worry about it. I'd have got the bus myself, but the 5.20 takes the scenic route. We're going out tonight and I won't get home in time."

"Ooo, doing something nice?"

Judy pressed the activate button on her phone and waited for the display to light up. "We're going to see a film at the Regal."

A wistful expression appeared on Beryl's face. "I haven't been to the pictures for ages."

"We don't go that often. But this one's been getting rave reviews so we thought we'd give it a whirl."

"What is it?"

Judy frowned at her phone. It hadn't come on. "I can't remember the title," she said, slightly distracted. "It's about frozen prehistoric creatures thawing out and terrorising a little village. Or something like that. I'm not that fussed to be honest, but you know Dave and his horror movies." She let out an exasperated sigh: "Bugger!"

"What's up, love?"

"Phone won't wake up. It's this damned battery. One minute it's fine, then it drops the charge in a blink." She sighed again. "Looks like I'll have to get the bus after all. We'll miss the adverts and the trailers – Dave won't be happy about that, he loves the trailers – but we should just about make the start of the film by the skin of our teeth."

"I feel awful now."

Judy smiled. "Don't be daft. It's not your fault."

Beryl rested her duster on the shelf and walked over to Judy. As if someone might be listening, she lowered her voice. "Why don't you just use the work phone, love?"

"Mrs Foster!" Judy exclaimed.

"What?" Beryl said, looking at her innocently.

Judy glared back at her as if to say 'you know what I mean'. "Are you trying to get me dragged across the coals? You know personal calls are a no-no. Head office has been really clamping down. Everything gets logged now."

"Yes, but they don't know what it's about, do they? For all they know it could be an emergency. I'd back you up if it ever got queried. Live dangerously. Just this once."

"I don't know…"

Beryl winked at her conspiratorially. "Go on. I won't tell anyone if you don't. And you are the manager after all."

"I don't think protesting that I'm the manager would wash with head office. I'm supposed to uphold the rules, not break them. But I suppose if I kept it short..."

Beryl laughed. "Go for it!"

"Trouble is, I'm not sure I can remember the number for Dave's mobile. 07737 52581... no, no hang on..."

Beryl rolled her eyes.

"07737 52571... no, that's not..." Judy's face lit up. "Ah! I think I've got it!"

Beryl stepped back over to the shelf and retrieved her duster. "That was painful to watch," she chuckled. "Go on, make your call. I'll keep watch for the phone call Gestapo."

Judy picked up the receiver from the phone beside the till and tapped in a number. "I don't know what it is with me and mobile numbers. I just can't keep them in my head. I can't even remember my own."

*

The tired, several decades out of date flocked wallpaper in Edwin Colthorpe's bedroom was almost entirely hidden by an impressive array of old western movie posters.

Slumped in an equally tired looking armchair, Edwin was immersed in a tattered paperback novel. His dark hair was dishevelled, flopping untidily out of place, and his baggy jumper – replete with a myriad of varying-sized holes – needed upgrading as badly as the wallpaper. His belt was hanging loose and his trousers hung open at the waist. He had his legs stretched out and his feet were rested on the edge of an unmade bed.

Edwin had had another bad day at work – nothing new there – and always found that immersing himself in a good western helped him escape from the drudgery of everyday life and salve his mental wounds.

A glimmer of daylight peeped through the closed curtains. The bulb in the bedside lamp, which provided Edwin with just about enough reading light, emitted little more than a dim glow.

He was so absorbed in the gunfight that was underway in his book that when the mobile phone on his bedside table first buzzed he barely even registered the noise. It was the light from the screen that caught his eye. He glanced over at it and frowned.

The only reason he owned a mobile phone was because everyone had them nowadays. But he seldom, if ever took calls on it, and had probably only ever sent one text. He used it instead for Internet access, but even that was minimal.

So who would be calling him now? He leaned over, picked up the phone and looked at the screen. Beneath the number on the display, the caller's location was identified as Eastbourne.

Edwin's frown deepened. Evidently it wasn't going to be anything of interest; he didn't know anyone in Eastbourne. Probably cold call sales then. He was about to return the phone to his bedside table when he suddenly thought better of it. If it was indeed a sales call and he didn't answer, they'd probably just keep calling back. He certainly didn't want that.

Ready to testily tell the caller to refrain from bothering him, he tapped the 'accept' option on the screen. "Hello?"

On the other end of the line, Judy was struggling to hold in a sneeze. "Hi. Beryl can't give me a lift tonight. Sorry it's short notice, but can you pick me up?"

Edwin hesitated. This wasn't what he'd expected.

Judy frowned. "Hello? Are you there?"

"Yes…"

"Well don't mess about. Can you pick me up?"

Edwin smiled and with a sudden spark of humour – which anyone who knew him would profess was distinctly alien to him – he chuckled, "Of course. It could be some time though, it looks like you're in Eastbourne and I'm in Rye."

Judy looked confused. "Rye? What on earth are you doing in…?" She stopped as the penny dropped. "Oh, is that you, Dave?"

"I'm afraid not, it appears you've called the wrong number."

Beryl was still busy dusting, making no secret of the fact she was listening in. She glanced over at Judy, who suddenly appeared to be very embarrassed.

"Oh, I'm terribly sorry to have disturbed you. Er... Have a nice evening."

Edwin put down his paperback book and eased back into his chair, as if settling down himself for a conversation with an old friend. "Please, you've nothing to apologise for. I do it all the time. I've royally embarrassed myself on more than one occasion."

Judy chuckled. "Haven't we all?"

Edwin was beginning to enjoy this conversation. It was so much better than having to deal with a salesman reading from a script. "I tell you, I get so many calls for nonsense like insurance for an accident I haven't had, or some phoney rebate from the bank. It's rather nice to have one from such a delightful lady. Even if it is an erroneous one."

Judy giggled slightly awkwardly. "That's very gracious of you. Thank you."

Edwin smiled with delight at the sound of the woman's laughter. "Well now, I suppose I'd better let you go. I hope you get your lift home safely. Of course, you can always call me back if you don't."

Judy laughed. "I'll keep that in mind. Thank you. And sorry again for bothering you. Goodbye."

As she hung up the receiver she noticed Beryl looking at her questioningly.

"Oh, I got the wrong number," Judy said, a little sheepishly. "I must have misdialled. The guy was very nice about it, but…"

"Were you flirting there, Mrs Harrison?"

Judy flushed slightly. "No I was *not*, Mrs Foster!" She paused and her eyes filled with a momentary far away look. "But he did sound very tasty." She laughed.

Edwin placed his phone back on the bedside table. He beamed with pleasure as he reflected upon what had just occurred. What a truly lovely sounding lady.

His little moment was abruptly shattered by a voice, shrieking at him from somewhere off in the house. "Edwin!"

*

Judy redialled Dave's number. "Second time lucky."

Beryl chuckled. "Surely you…"

Judy raised a 'shhh' finger as a voice sounded on the end of the line. This time she thought it best to test the water first. "Dave?"

Her face relaxed. "Is there any chance you can you come and collect me after work? Beryl can't bring me home tonight." She paused, then smiled and nodded at her colleague. "Thanks. Is there…" She paused again. "No, I'm using the shop phone. I think my mobile has died. Is there any chance we can drop Beryl home too?" A pause. Then she gave Beryl a quick thumbs-up. "Okay. See you soon." Another pause. "Love you too." She replaced the receiver.

Beryl smiled. "All sorted?"

"Yes, he'll be here just after five. And we can drop you home too."

"Thank you, love. Only if it won't make you late for your film."

"It won't."

"You've got yourself a keeper there."

Judy smiled warmly. "Yeah. I have."

CHAPTER 3

The following morning, Edwin – with a satchel slung across his back and whistling cheerily – cycled to work on his father's old pushbike. The minimal remaining paintwork discernible on the frame was a dulled maroon colour and both rusted mudguards rattled irritatingly, the volume increasing and decreasing commensurate with how hard he pedalled. He'd often thought about replacing it, but his mother had made her feelings on the matter abundantly clear: "It was your father's and while the wheels are still turning you'll use it and be grateful for small mercies."

Edwin negotiated a sharp turn from Tower Street onto Conduit Hill and pedalled as fast as he could down to the High Street. Half way along he scooted into the small courtyard adjacent to the private rental office block where he worked and hopped off, noting with some pleasure that, aside from Ian – whose Ford Focus was neatly parked up in one corner, and who always arrived at an unfeasibly early hour – he was going to be first in. He wheeled the bike past Ian's car and over to the solitary lamppost beside the wall. Withdrawing a padlock and a heavy-duty link-chain from his satchel, he bent down and secured the bike to the post. It was unlikely anyone would give a second look to a bike that patently belonged on the tip, let alone deign to steal it but Edwin never took that chance. He rattled the lock to make sure it was secure and, patting a loose strand of his thickly Brylcreem'd hair back into place, he trotted into the nearby doorway.

Whistling, he sprinted up the narrow staircase, taking the steps two at a time. At the top he turned right and passed through a swing door, over which a brass plaque was mounted: *East Sussex Spectator*.

As Edwin walked into the office, the *Spectator*'s editor, Ian Hunt, looked up from the pile of paperwork on his desk. He pushed his octagonal spectacles up on his head and glanced up at the clock over the doorway. His round face adopted a quizzical look. "First in, Ed? What happened, did you shit the bed?"

"No!" Edwin rebuked as he walked across to his desk in the corner beside the window. It was a common enough expression and certainly uttered without malice. Yet repeated childhood accidents can leave deep scars – especially when they resulted in a stiff thrashing with the back of a clothes brush from an unsympathetic parent – and Edwin always bristled at it. Hoping to hide the hurt in his eyes, he forced a smile. "Just thought I'd make an early start. I'm a bit down on my target and after today I'll be off for the rest of the week."

Ian adjusted his rolled up shirt sleeves, slipped his spectacles back into place and returned to the documentation in front of him. "Good man," he muttered.

Two words. Two simple words. But it wasn't often that Ian spoke kindly to him and Edwin would take every crumb he could get. His forced smile melted into something genuinely appreciative and, resuming his whistling, he sat down and switched on his laptop.

Ian peered theatrically at him over the rim of his spectacles. First in *and* whistling cheerfully? What was going on with Edwin this morning?

The door opened and a tall, auburn haired woman attired in a sharp two-piece business suit marched in. "Morning."

Ian didn't look up. "Morning, Ally."

Edwin broke off his whistling and smiled at her. "Morning." Then he resumed his slightly out of tune warbling.

Alysson Baines had worked for the *Spectator* since its inception seven years earlier. Since then, you could probably have counted the days on one hand that she wasn't first in to the office. She smiled at Edwin with surprise. "Someone's in a good mood this morning."

Ian looked up and peered over his spectacles. "Yes, I was thinking just now that's a distinct cat who got the cream refrain. Do I detect the mood of a man who got lucky last night? What do you say, Ed?

Alysson looked intrigued. She raised her eyebrows at Edwin. "*Really?* Anyone we know Ed?"

Edwin ignored them and started sifting through his email inbox. But the trace of a smile on his lips hinted that he secretly rather liked the idea his co-workers might think he was in a sexual relationship with someone.

Ian and Allyson exchanged grins as she crossed to her desk. "Did Simon and Will sort out the copy I left for them last night?"

Ian sat back in his chair and pushed his spectacles up onto his forehead. "You know designers, sweetheart. You'd have heard quickly enough if there were any issues. Oh, and while I'm thinking about it, Terry and Carrie have gone out to get a story on the opening of that new care home. I'd suggest it's worth getting on the blower to their promotions department and pumping them for some advertising."

Alysson switched on her laptop. "I'll get on it right away."

Ian looked over at Ed. "Weren't you supposed to be dealing with that one?"

"Alysson is welcome to try. I got in touch with them last week." Edwin looked over at a post-it note stuck on the wall beside his desk. "A woman named Julia Fitch deals with their advertising. But she ran me round the houses a bit. She said she'd call me back, but she didn't. I tried several times over a couple of days, but every time she was 'in a meeting'.

I think they're hoping we'll run the story first then they won't actually need to *pay* for anything."

Ian shook his head. "Buggers will try it on, won't they?" He sighed. "Well, they can hope all they like. We'll give the opening event a couple of paragraphs, but if they want something more expansive they're going to have to dip into their advertising budget."

Alysson nodded. "Absolutely."

The door opened again and a good-looking young man in a tightly-fitted pinstripe suit, swaggered in. "Mornin' Ally cat. Mornin' boss..." He trailed off as he noticed Edwin. "Fuck me, shit the bed, Ed?"

Edwin's cheerful demeanour evaporated. He didn't like Blake Dean. He never had done and never would do. It wasn't just that, no matter how much he played the office fool, Blake managed to consistently top Edwin's sales figure. No, there was far more to it that that, his very being irked Edwin greatly.

Having made it clear that that he didn't appreciate Blake's filthy language, it was like red rag to a bull, and he often became the target for a frequent maelstrom of obscene ribbing. He'd regretted having let slip that he didn't approve, but of course it was now way too late. Yet perhaps worse than any of that, Blake always spoke about women with an insulting derisory regard and almost everything the man said made Edwin simply boil inside.

"I already told Ian, I did no such thing," he said, stone-faced.

Blake grinned triumphantly. He had elicited exactly the reaction he wanted. He looked over at Alysson. "Make yourself useful, love. Pop the kettle on. I'm absolutely gagging for it!" He winked at her.

Although she rolled her eyes, the trace of a smile hinted that Alysson rather enjoyed the sexual innuendo spouted by this younger man. She got up and went over to the coffee pot sitting on a percolator beside the window. "Lucky for you I was just going to get one for myself, or I'd have told you to do one."

Blake grinned cheekily and stepped over to his desk. "Thanks, Ally cat. You know I appreciate everything you do for me. And I do mean *everything*." He sat down on his chair and, using his feet to propel himself, he wheeled the chair on its casters towards Edwin, moving his hands backwards and forwards in the air as if manipulating the wheels on a wheelchair. "Nothing better than lubricating your lips with something hot and wet first thing in the morning, ain't that right Eduardo?"

Edwin kept his eyes fixed firmly on his laptop screen. "Don't be so vulgar."

Blake struggled to withhold a snigger. "Yeah, sorry. S'pose you wouldn't really know much about that, would you? Getting your tongue…"

Alysson snapped. "Ed's right, don't be so damned bloody vulgar!"

Chortling, Blake waggled his eyebrows at her. He pushed his chair backwards a few feet, again childishly using his hands to make as if he was manoeuvring a wheelchair. He glanced at the sales board on the wall. "Blimey, I should've taken the day off. I'm well over target for the week already."

Ian stood up and ambled over to Blake. He slapped him heartily on the shoulder. "Well done, lad. Don't know what the *Spectator* would do without you."

Blake grinned smugly. "Thanks, boss."

Edwin quietly bristled and refocused his attention on his computer screen.

Ian gripped the back of Blake's chair and began to wheel him back over to his desk. "But if you want to stay my number one boy you'd better get on and do some work."

"Sure thing, boss man." Blake glanced up at the sales board and noticed Edwin's figure. It was well below his own. Adopting a tone of mock concern, he said, "Oh, no! Not lookin' so good, Ed!"

Ian deposited Blake at his desk and turned just as Alysson came over with a mug of coffee. She handed it to Blake. "Ian?"

"No thanks, sweetheart. I had one when I got in." Ian walked back to his desk. "I'll have another one mid-morning."

As Alysson went back to collect her own mug, Blake licked the rim of his coffee cup and waggled his eyebrows at her.

"Dream on," she said. But again there was a momentary flicker that perhaps revealed her inner feelings about the flirtatious Blake Dean.

Blake grinned. "Yeah, you know you want it." Putting on a robotic voice, he added, "Resistance is futile. Resistance is futile."

Alysson rolled her eyes. "Stupid child!" she said, with unconvincing disdain.

Blake smirked and took a big mouthful of coffee. "Ahhhhhh. Hot and wet. Nothing else quite like it." He set the mug down and clapped his hands together. "Right, let's get this show on the road – make us some moolah!"

CHAPTER 4

It wasn't quite 11 o'clock and already the heat of the day had become unbearable. Although the door of the St Joshua's Hospice Charity shop was wedged wide open with a rubber doorstop, the benefits were proving negligible.

Judy had a pile of DVDs tucked into the crook of her arm and was trying to create some space for them on a rotating rack which was already heaving with stock.

Beryl was serving a customer at the till. There seemed to be an issue with a pair of gloves the elderly man had purchased and it was proving difficult to make him understand they were irreplaceable. "We only had the one pair, Sir," Beryl explained patiently.

"So you definitely can't exchange them?"

"Not like for like. They were a donation. We do have several other different pairs if you wanted to…"

The man waved his hand dismissively. "No, no, I wanted these."

Beryl peered at the offending spot on one of the gloves. "It's only a small mark. But if you're not happy I can give you a refund."

The man frowned, pondering the options. "I'd rather have another pair the same."

"I'd like to be able to help, but it's this pair or the refund, I'm afraid."

The man reached a decision. "I suppose I'll just have to keep them then," he mumbled grumpily. "I think a slight discount would be equitable though."

Beryl shot a slightly exasperated glance at Judy. "They only cost a pound, sir."

The man was clearly getting agitated now. "Oh, very well. But I shan't be buying anything in here again!" He snatched up the gloves and left the shop.

"Some people!" Beryl exclaimed, shaking her head in disbelief.

"He'll be back," Judy laughed. "You know Frank's been coming in here for years and it's pretty much a guarantee he will come back to complain about everything he has bought. He wouldn't be Frank if he didn't. It's a favourite pastime for him."

"Oh, I know. But why would anyone complain about a tiny speck on a practically brand new pair of gloves that only cost a pound? They're lovely quality and they must have been at least £20 originally. If he wants to find something to complain about, at least make it something worthwhile."

Judy laughed again as she squeezed another DVD onto the display rack. "Like I say, that's Frank for you."

Another of the shop's elderly volunteers, Sylvia Bassett, appeared from the back room carrying a pile of dresses. "Where would you like these, Judy?"

"If you could put them on hangers and slip a size cube on each of them that'd be great."

A twinkle appeared in Beryl's eye. "Hey, Sylv, I meant to tell you, Judy's got a new boyfriend."

Judy pulled a face. "Get on with your work, Mrs Foster. And stop stirring it!"

Beryl giggled mischievously. Sylvia's face lit up and her eyes widened excitedly. "Ooooo." She threw the pile of dresses over the top of the rack and walked over to the counter. "Come on then, dish the goss!"

Judy sighed. "Don't listen to our resident fantasist. It was something and nothing. I had to phone Dave just before we closed yesterday. I misdialled and ended up talking to some guy. And now Beryl's ordering the wedding cake!"

"Well, you were chattering away to him. And you did say he sounded tasty."

"I'd hardly call it chattering away. I was just being polite." Judy smiled coquettishly. "But yes, I won't deny it, he did sound nice."

Beryl grinned. "Well there you go then."

Sylvia pouted. "Awww, all the fun stuff happens when I'm not here. What would Dave say if he knew?"

Dave suddenly appeared behind them through the open shop door. "If Dave knew what?"

Startled by his sudden appearance from nowhere, all three women looked as if they'd just been caught with their hands in the cookie jar.

"Morning, ladies."

"Morning." Beryl and Sylvia chimed in unison.

Judy looked a little confused to see her husband. "Hello love. What...?" She trailed off as she saw her lunchbox clutched in Dave's hand. "Oh!"

Dave crossed the shop, leant across between the women – "Excuse me, ladies." – and placed the box on the counter beside the till. "Dave's delivery service. One forgotten lunchbox."

"Aw, thanks, love. I was going to pop out and get a sandwich."

"So, come on then." Dave looked at the three women enquiringly. "What did I miss? If Dave knew *what*?"

Judy looked a little awkward. Thinking quickly she said, "Oh, er... if you knew I was about to have a big slice of chocolate cake with my coffee."

Dave smiled. "He'd say 'Enjoy it'." He gave Judy a quick peck on the cheek. "Well, don't let me interrupt your coffee morning ladies." He looked at Judy. "See you tonight."

Judy walked him to the door. "Thanks for bringing my lunch. Don't know where my head was this morning."

"That's okay, there's no charge." He smiled lovingly at his wife. "'cept a kiss."

They quickly kissed goodbye and Dave strolled out into the sunshine.

Judy turned round as Beryl and Sylvia burst out laughing. "Right you two troublemakers. "*You*," she pointed at Sylvia, "get those dresses cubed and racked. And *you*," she pulled an angry face at Beryl, "there's a donation out back that needs sorting before lunch. So hop to it!"

*

Edwin sat staring intently up at the clock above the door of the *Spectator* office. There was no sign of Alysson and Ian was frantically tapping away at his keyboard. As the second hand swept past the 12, completing what in Edwin's opinion had been an excruciatingly long journey to 3 o'clock, he clicked the 'shut down' option on his laptop and began to hurriedly pack up his satchel.

From across the office Blake was watching Edwin with an amused look on his face. "Bit of a hurry to get out, Ed? Hot date tonight?"

Edwin knew it was futile to engage Blake in conversation, but he replied anyway. "What I do in my own time has absolutely nothing to do with you," he said tersely.

Blake pulled an exaggerated face. "Alright, alright, Mr Stroppy. Calm down. Just askin'. So, er... have you?"

"Have I *what*?"

"Got a hot date lined up. A bit of snatch?"

Edwin didn't even qualify that with a reply. He stood up and slung his satchel over his shoulder. "Goodnight, Ian."

In typical Ian fashion, he didn't look up. "Bye. Enjoy your time off."

"Thanks. I will."

As Edwin crossed the office, Blake grinned up at him. "'Ere, I've got a joke for you. You'll like this one. How is sex like air?"

Edwin walked past without acknowledging him. Blake smirked. "It's not a big deal unless you aren't getting any!" He guffawed.

As Edwin walked out, Blake shouted out after him. "Cheerio, Eduardo!"

Edwin reached the top of the staircase outside the office and stopped as he saw Alysson coming up. He stepped aside to let her pass.

"Thank you. Have a nice evening, Ed. And well done for making target today. See you in the morning."

Edwin liked Alysson. She was the only person in the office that made his day bearable. "Afraid not," he said with a hint of mock disappointment. "Sadly I shan't be in again till Monday. Oh, wait... did I say *sadly*?" He beamed at her with a distinct self satisfaction.

Alysson smiled back. "Lucky you! Well, whatever you're doing, have fun."

"Thanks. I will."

Alysson disappeared back into the office through the swing door and Edwin skittered happily down the stairs. But as he emerged from the office block doorway, he stopped abruptly and his face fell.

A shiny BMW – *Blake's* shiny BMW – was parked unnecessarily close to the lamppost, making it extremely difficult for Edwin to access his bike. Why was he surprised that the thoughtless oaf would do this? Thoughtless? No, Edwin decided. This was intentional. *Again.*

He huffed and made his way round to the far side of the vehicle, just managing to squeeze past, and bent down to get at the padlock. With difficulty, and taking the skin off the back of his hand in the process, he managed to get the lock off and pulled the chain out. The end of the chain whipped up and missed the door of the BMW by millimetres. Edwin winced. Then again, it would have served that moron right if his precious car *had* been damaged.

Looking decidedly flustered, Edwin tucked the lock and chain into his satchel and carefully wheeled the bike out from behind the car. Slinging the satchel across his back, he hopped on and took off out of the courtyard.

As he cycled along, Edwin felt his annoyance melting away and he started to pedal faster. Four days off work now. It didn't get much better than that. Except that *this* four-day break was going to be something rather special. He began to whistle cheerfully.

In the road up ahead there was a car struggling to get into a parking space that was clearly too small, and Edwin slowed down to a crawl. As he did so, he noticed the clothing store in the middle of the row of shops across the street. He stopped his bike, climbed off and wheeled it to the edge of the pavement.

Above the shop window was an ornately hand-painted sign displaying the words 'Hamlisch & Martin: Gentlemen's Couturier' in an Old English font.

An independent store, Hamlisch & Martin had been a fixture in Rye for decades and, as a child, Edwin had accompanied his father inside on several occasions. Kindly old Mr Hamlisch – who must have been pushing 80 then, and was now long since dead – always gave Edwin a toffee from the jar he kept under the counter. He smiled at the memory as he stood looking at the mannequins in the window. The display was very much designed to attract 'the modern man', and his eyes lit up as he admired a particularly sharp looking outfit. Hamlisch & Martin weren't a cheap option; far from it. But in terms of quality garments and guarunteed excellent service there were few better retailers. At least, not in Rye.

Edwin wheeled his bike over to a nearby parking meter and chained it up. Casting a bemused glance at the driver who was *still* refusing to accept that his car was never going to fit into that space, he strolled confidently into the shop.

CHAPTER 5

It was almost 5.00pm when Edwin finally reached home. With an olive green paper carrier bag embossed with Hamlisch & Martin's logo swinging on its gold cord handles from the handlebars, he pedalled his pushbike up the short driveway that fronted the ageing red brick property where he'd lived since birth.

He climbed off in front of the garage that abutted the house. Sliding the carrier bag off the handlebars, he placed it on the ground beside the old, part-wood-part-brick construction. He pulled a bunch of keys from his pocket, unlocked the twin doors, pulled open the left hand one and wheeled the bike in. Leaning it carefully against the wall, he went back outside. He retrieved the carrier bag, then he stepped back in, swung the door shut behind him and locked up, rattling the doors just to be certain.

The internal side door leading to the kitchen was open and he slipped quietly through. He stopped just inside, listening. Satisfied he'd not been heard, he stealthily crossed the kitchen and went out into the hall. Noting that the stairlift was at the bottom of the stairs – she must be in the sitting room, he thought – Edwin rested the carrier bag on the small utility table just inside the front door and removed his shoes. As quietly as possible he placed them on the rack beneath the table and crept across the bare floorboards towards the staircase.

As he set one foot on the bottom step, it creaked and a voice called out from the sitting room.

"Is that you, Edwin?"

Wincing, Edwin stopped. "I'll be through in a moment. I'm just going upstairs to change."

As he began to ascend the staircase an ear-assailing scraping and clunking sound emanated from the sitting room. "Just a moment."

Edwin stopped halfway up the stairs, gritted his teeth and hastily tried to tuck the clothing store bag out of sight.

Hunched over a walker, Constance Colthorpe appeared in the doorway of the sitting room. She was wearing a long cardigan that, much like Edwin's own limited wardrobe, had seen better days, underneath which was a pair of loose-fitting pyjama bottoms and a white t-shirt bearing a discernible brown stain.

Edwin stared at the stain with barely concealed revulsion – oxtail soup by the looks of it, he thought. "You didn't get dressed today, Mother."

Constance clunked her walker a few more steps out into the hall and came to a halt, glaring up at her son. "No, I didn't feel like it," she replied testily. "And if I don't feel like it I don't have to."

"But surely you'd feel so much better if…" Edwin began.

Constance snapped. "Never you mind what I'm wearing. You're late. Where have you been?"

"Oh, I, er…" Edwin glanced down to make sure his Hamlisch & Martin purchase was tucked out of sight behind his legs. "I was held up at work."

"Held up at work?" Constance scoffed. "A likely story. Doing *what?*"

Edwin ignored the question. "I'll just pop upstairs and change, and then I'll get dinner started."

The mention of dinner instantly averted any further questions about her son's whereabouts. "Well don't take all night," Constance grumbled. "I'm hungry."

Managing to manipulate the carrier bag to keep it out of sight of Constance's prying eyes, Edwin turned and hurried on up the stairs. "I'll be down when I'm down," he said under his breath.

Constance stared up after him. "What are you saying? Stop mumbling, you incoherent boy!"

"Back in a jiffy, Mother." At the top of the stairs, Edwin moved Constance's dedicated *upstairs* walker neatly to one side and disappeared through the door into his bedroom.

Constance tutted to herself. "He'd let me starve to death, I swear he would." She turned her walker and clunked noisily back into the sitting room.

*

Aside from 'The Happy Wok' – a Chinese takeaway that had been shut down twice in the past three years under orders from the Food Standards Agency – 'AberaKebabera', two doors along, was the only takeaway business in Rye that didn't specialise in fish and chips. With its dubious claim of providing the townsfolk of Rye with 'the very finest in Turkish cuisine', 'AberaKebabera' had been on Cyprus Place for years and the pungent, lingering odour of doner had taken up residence in the walls of the small bedsit above the premises; the sparsely furnished bedsit where Blake Dean was preparing for yet another evening of solitude.

The late afternoon temperature was still up around 23 degrees as he stripped off his pinstripe suit and tossed it on the floor. He didn't bother to redress. Clutching his mobile phone, and wearing nothing but a pair of crumpled polka dot boxers, he went over to the kitchenette, opened the fridge and took out a bottle of Heineken. He stood for a moment holding it against his brow, luxuriating in the exquisite coolness. Then he went over to the small worktop, switched on the kettle and opened up the cupboard underneath. Surveying the dozen or more plastic tubs of noodles stacked inside, he selected one labelled Singapore Super-Hot and peeled off the foil lid. While he waited for the kettle to boil, he crossed to the two-seater sofa, put down his mobile phone on the small table and retrieved the TV remote that was wedged between the sofa arm and a scatter cushion.

Blake's 52-inch high definition, widescreen television was his pride and joy, second only in his affections to the BMW, which itself, despite the fact he'd bragged to anyone who'd listen he'd bought outright, was still only partially his; it'd be another seven years before he'd completely paid it off, at a not inconsiderable rate of interest. He pressed the 'power' button on the remote and the TV woke up. The game station underneath the set was already on, he'd dozed off on the sofa the previous evening and, having to rush to work, he'd not even thought about switching it off when he left. The screen filled with a virtual-world, a mountainous vista of some far off planet with a tangerine sky.

The kettle boiled and Blake dropped the remote on the sofa, set down his Heineken on the table alongside and returned to the worktop. He poured the hot water into the tub of noodles, cursing under his breath as he misjudged the fill level and it spilled over the side. He picked up a fork, quickly inspected it, and – deciding that traces of yesterday's baked bean sauce weren't going to do him any harm – he stuck it in the tub and crossed back to the sofa, vigorously stirring the noodles as he went.

There wasn't much veracity in the Blake Dean that he presented to the world. He'd spent his entire life building a persona that couldn't have been further from the *real* him if it tried. In his very first year at school he'd discovered that popularity could be bought with humour and he'd rapidly forged a reputation as the class joker. It hadn't done much for his education – 'Needs to concentrate more on his studies and less on amusing his classmates' became something of a prerequisite on his annual reports – but, despite the ear-bashing it had earned him at home, he hadn't cared. Being liked had been far more important to him than being smart.

As is the way, when Blake got older he'd discovered girls; the problem was, they never really discovered him. Sure, that twinkle in his eye and ribald sense of humour made them laugh, but it hadn't encouraged any of them to open their legs. For the entire duration of his teenage years, he'd found gratification either from imagining well-developed classroom flirt Tina Reynolds with no clothes on, or in the company of top shelf magazines and a box of supersoft tissues.

His first real experience with the opposite sex – a fumble outside a nightclub two years ago, just after he'd turned 23 – had come to a messy end when he'd prematurely climaxed over the girl's jeans and she'd literally punched him in the face, chipping one of his incisors, and stormed off back inside. He'd subsequently found an outlet for his urges with local prostitutes. He'd only had one bad experience when a pock-faced girl calling herself Jade had laughed hysterically at first sight of his distinctly underdeveloped manhood. He'd failed to get aroused, but she'd demanded he stump up the cash anyway: "You got a handful of tit, didn't ya? Ya can fuckin' well pay for it, or my boyfriend will fuck you up big time!" After that, Blake had made sure he never again ventured anywhere near the area where he'd picked her up. The women he did patronise weren't exactly the sort he loudly and proudly bragged about having spent the night with – one of them was probably old enough to be his mother – but they were good sorts and he'd become a regular with two of them, Marcia and Cheryl, neither of whom had any hang-ups about catering to his outré requests.

On the way home that afternoon, Blake had thought he might hook up with one of his favourite ladies for the evening. But now, stretching back on the sofa and tucking into his noodles, he decided he really couldn't be bothered. It was too hot anyway for the usual messy stuff.

He shovelled the last of the noodles into his mouth, ran the back of his hand across his chin and wiped the residue down his boxers. He drained the bottle of lager, then got up and went back to the kitchenette. Tossing the empty noodle tub into the sink, he got himself another Heineken from the fridge. His crotch was itching again; he really needed to speak to the pharmacist about it, it had been driving him crazy since last Saturday's disastrous encounter with the drunken Siobhan. Scratching at himself, he sauntered back to the sofa and set about single-handedly blasting the 'Krolox', cannibal alien beings that had tricked him into landing on their planet back in level three. After an hour of game station mayhem, he decided he did need to release some tension after all. Teasing Ed about orally pleasuring women had been playing on his mind all day and he was feeling a little bit horny.

Standing up, he walked over to the window and looked down on the street below. The evening crowd were beginning to show their faces and it would only be a matter of time before all the eateries and swanky wine bars in the street were filled to capacity. He pulled the curtains, returned to the sofa and sat down. Picking up his mobile phone, he scrolled through his list of contacts. He tapped on a number and waited for an answer. "Hello, Marcia?" he said, slipping a hand under the elastic of his boxer shorts. "I don't half fancy a bit of dirty talk."

*

Judy, Dave and their teenage son Chris were gathered at the dining room table having their evening meal. Judy had made a fresh lasagne. It was Dave's favourite and although it would never have been her first choice on a menu, she didn't mind cooking it occasionally. Chris, on the other hand, was impossible to please and he was sitting – headphones firmly adhered to his ears – picking at the food on his plate.

"Good day at college, love?" Judy mouthed at him. Getting no response, she motioned to her son to take off the headphones.

He caught her out of the corner of his eye and lifted them away from his ear on one side. "Did you have a good day at college?" she asked again.

Chris shrugged. "It was alright I s'pose." He dropped the headphone back onto his ear and returned his attention to the business of not actually eating his meal.

Dave finished his last mouthful, pushed his plate away and sat back with a satisfied expression on his face. "Very nice. Thanks, love."

Judy smiled. "There's a little bit more in the kitchen if you'd like it."

Dave patted his stomach. "No, I'm done. Got to watch my figure."

Judy stood up, picked up her husband's plate and placed it on top of her own. She motioned to Chris to get his attention. "Are you finished with that?"

He reluctantly lifted the headphone away from his ear. "Huh?"

"Have you finished eating, love?"

"Oh, yeah. Thanks." He handed Judy the plate.

Judy took it from him and walked through to the kitchen.

Dave picked up his glass of water and drained it. "I spotted Don in town this morning. I haven't seen him for months."

"How is he?" Judy called from the kitchen.

"We didn't actually speak. He was crossing the street up the way. Just after I left you this morning at the shop."

Judy reappeared in the dining room doorway. "Thanks again for dropping my lunch in. I don't know how I forgot to put it in my bag. I must have been in a daydream this morning."

Dave looked at her and chuckled. "You were probably preoccupied thinking about that big old chunk of chocolate cake."

Judy frowned. "Chocolate cake?"

"Yeah, the one you were going to have with your coffee this morning."

A slightly awkward expression appeared on Judy's face. She hated lying to Dave. She didn't even know why she'd said what she had. It wasn't as if there was anything to feel guilty about. It had been completely innocent, a stupid misdialled phone call. But she regretted saying to Beryl that the man on the end of the line had sounded nice, then she'd been caught off guard by Dave's sudden appearance and the little white lie had just slipped out. She averted her eyes. "Oh, that…"

"Yeah. Did it live up to anticipation?"

Judy turned and walked back into the kitchen. As non-committal as possible she simply responded with an "Hmmm."

*

The moment he'd got to his room, Edwin had stripped off his work suit, dropped it on the floor and eagerly withdrawn his new outfit from the carrier bag. Fashion had never featured high among his list of priorities. As far as he was concerned clothing was functional, nothing more. And, in his opinion, people who spent a fortune to fill a wardrobe with fripperies they'd probably only ever wear once had more money than sense. This was the first time in his life that he'd purchased something he believed was commonly referred to as 'smart casual'. Despite the Hamlisch & Martin salesman's persuasive assurance as to otherwise, he hadn't been entirely convinced that a pale blue herringbone jacket suited him. Yet now, as he stood admiring his new look in the three-quarter length mirror attached to the back of the bedroom door, as accompaniment to the crisp white cotton shirt and slim-fit beige linen slacks, he had to admit that it had been money well spent.

He gently patted his hair into place, pushed back his shoulders and turned to the left, and then the right. There was no doubt about it; he did look rather splendid. He'd never put much stock in the claim that everyone has a best side. As far as he was concerned both his sides were completely unremarkable. But as he stood inspecting himself in the mirror, there was no doubt in his mind that a proverb he recalled from those tedious Latin classes at school – *vetis virum facit* – held more truth than he'd ever given it credence.

"Clothes maketh the man," he murmured, nodding approvingly at his reflection. He glanced down at his feet. The tan leather brogues might have been a little profligate at £185, but looking at them now they truly *were* the icing on the cake.

He crossed to the bedside table and picked up his mobile phone. Tapping the icon to access his recent calls he stared intently at the Eastbourne number on the screen. He closed his eyes as if trying to commit it to memory, but as he did so Constance's voice screeched at him from off downstairs. "Edwin, what are you doing up there? Stop lollygagging around. If I don't eat soon you know very well that I'll get a bout of my troubles again!"

Edwin returned his phone to the table. "Just coming, Mother." He hastily undressed, carefully folded his new clothes and tucked them back into the carrier bag. Then he threw on a sweater and a faded pair of chinos and went downstairs.

The quiet, rhythmic ticking of the grandfather clock was the only sound in the sitting room. Constance, sat by the fireplace in an armchair with its back to the door, was pondering the partially completed jigsaw puzzle on the table in front of her. She had a piece in her hand and a pinched expression on her lips as she squinted intently at the partially completed picture of two New Forest ponies in woodland.

Edwin entered the room quietly. With a disdainful grimace on his face, he approached his mother. He stepped round the side of the chair, casting a faint shadow over her jigsaw.

Constance looked up sharply. "About time too!"

"Dinner then?"

"Of course dinner! What's the matter with you, you feckless boy?"

Edwin forced a smile. "Liver and onions okay?"

Constance glared at him as if she were dealing with a halfwit. "Why are you even asking me that?" she said incredulously. "We discussed it last night. Just get on with it." She flapped a bony hand at him. "And get out of the blasted light, I can't see my jigsaw puzzle properly."

Edwin leaned forward and peered down at it. "That's nice," he ventured.

"No it *isn't*," she snapped. "It's nothing but bracken. Bracken, bracken and more bracken. What possible chance have I got of finishing it when it all looks the same?"

"That's the challenge, Mother. The fun."

"*Fun*?! Oh, hark at mister clever clogs. Do you want to do it?" She held out one of the offending jigsaw pieces. "Well, *do* you?"

Edwin turned away. "I'll get dinner on."

As he walked through to the kitchen, Constance called after him, "And don't burn the onions like you did last time!"

Edwin opened the fridge door, took out a plate of liver covered in cling-film and a couple of onions and nudged the door shut with his bottom. He set the food down on the worktop and, whistling cheerfully, lifted down a frying pan from the cupboard and placed it on the hotplate atop the Aga cooker. He pulled out a chopping board and placed it on the table. Fetching a knife from the drawer, he slowly set about chopping up an onion.

Constance shouted through to him. "Stop that dreadful chirruping. You sound like a canary! And chop faster, boy! Chop, chop, chop!! I want my dinner tonight, not tomorrow! Can't you do *anything* right?"

Edwin immediately stopped whistling. He stared down at the chopping board. Then, taking a deep breath, he closed his eyes.

With a sudden lightning movement, he grabbed up half of the unchopped onion and marched across the kitchen back into the living room. He strode angrily across towards Constance and kicked over the little table, sending pieces of her jigsaw flying in all directions. Waving the kitchen knife aggressively, his Brylcreem'd hair flapping wildly, with astonishing ferocity he thrust the onion right up under the cowering woman's nose.

"Do you want to fucking do it then? Well, *do* you? You shrivelled up, impatient old *cunt*!" His eyes blazed with hatred as he raised the knife, his knuckles turning a pale white as he tightened his grip on the haft.

Constance stared up at him, her eyes brimming with tears and her face etched with a combination of stark terror and pleading. "Please, Edwin, no! I'm sorry. I didn't mean to seem so ungrateful. I love you, son. I…"

Edwin's eyes snapped open as he emerged from his little reverie.

Letting out a resigned sigh, he resumed chopping the onion. Perhaps a little faster now. "Going as quick as I can, Mother," he called apologetically.

CHAPTER 6

At a little before 9 o'clock the following morning, Edwin was standing in front of the mirror, once again attired in his spiffy new outfit. His hair was freshly slicked with Brylcreem and coiffure'd to perfection.

Classical music emanated from a small transistor radio on top of his chest of drawers, filling the room. Edwin hummed along to it.

Quite the catch, he thought, as he adjusted the collar on his jacket and smiled at his reflection.

Turning the volume on the radio down to almost inaudible, he picked up his phone from the bedside table and sat back in his armchair. He tapped at the screen and called up the Eastbourne number. He withdrew a folded handkerchief from his trouser pocket and dabbed at his damp hands. He'd felt so confident about this, but now the moment had come he suddenly felt extremely nervous. Taking a deep breath, he tapped the 'call back' option.

When the phone rang in the St Joshua's Hospice Charity shop, Sylvia was in the midst of sorting through a selection of garments on a clothing rack. Judy was unlocking the door to open up. She looked over at Sylvia.

Sylvia smiled. "I'll get it." She crossed to the counter and picked up the receiver.

"Good morning, St Joshua's Hospice, Eastbourne," she said in a sing-songy manner.

Edwin's face flickered with disappointment; this wasn't the same lady he'd spoken to on Tuesday afternoon. "Oh, good morning," he said cheerfully.

"I was just calling to enquire on your shops opening times today."

"We're open Monday to Saturday, from nine o'clock to four thirty in the afternoon."

"Thank you very much indeed." Edwin tapped the screen to end call his call and let out a sigh of relief. That wasn't so hard after all. Nothing to be nervous about. It was just a shame that it wasn't the same delightful woman he'd spoken to a couple of days ago. He tapped at his phone again to access Google and in the search field entered 'St Joshua's Hospice, Eastbourne'. He smiled with satisfaction as the address promptly popped up on the screen.

Getting up, he slung a rucksack over his shoulder and walked out of his bedroom, closing the door behind him. He squeezed past the stairlift at the top of the staircase and began to descend. Almost immediately the familiar grating scrape-clunk scrape-clunk sound of Constance's walker sounded on the upstairs landing.

"Who were you talking to in there?"

Annoyed, Edwin stopped halfway down the stairs. How could she have possibly heard that? He was only on the phone for 20 seconds. As he turned, Constance – attired in a lavender winceyette nightgown with a crocheted shawl draped across her shoulders – appeared menacingly at the top of the stairs.

"It was just a friend," Edwin said.

"*What* friend?" his mother replied scornfully. "You haven't got any friends." She peered at him inquisitively. "And why are you all dressed up like a dog's dinner? What's going on?"

"I'm going away for a few days, Mother."

Constance looked at him, a little bemused. "You're what? Don't be so *ridiculous*. What do you mean, going away?"

"Going away. Taking a break from…"

"From *what*? Go on, say it, boy. Don't be shy. Me I suppose!"

To the observant, Edwin's expression might have disclosed a definitive 'too damned right', but with equanimity he replied, "Of course not. A break from work. I'm meeting a friend. It's only for a couple of days. I'll be back for dinner on Sunday."

"I thought you'd taken time off work specifically to redecorate the bathroom."

"That was the original plan. But something else has come up," Edwin exclaimed cheerfully. "The bathroom can wait," he added.

Constance's expression changed. Here comes the sympathy card, Edwin thought. "But what will *I* do?" Constance said, with as calculatingly feeble an inflection as she could muster.

"What will I eat? You can't just leave me here on my own. Please, Edwin."

Edwin was unfazed. He'd seen it all before. First the 'pity poor me', he thought. And then, when things didn't go her way, would come the outrage.

"I prepared you some breakfast first thing," he said. "It's on the kitchen table. And there are plenty of meals to choose from in the fridge, you can pop whatever you fancy into the microwave."

Constance's eyes widened in horror and her indignation returned. "You know I can't use that dreadful thing," she snapped. "It frightens me!"

Edwin turned away and walked on down the stairs. As he passed Constance's downstairs walker, he dutifully moved it to give her easier access to it when she came down. "It's just a microwave, Mother," he called back up to her. "You'll be perfectly fine. If you're really desperate you can always telephone Mrs Baker."

Constance's face filled with rage. "How *dare* you walk away from me when I'm talking to you, boy?" she screeched furiously. "Come back here this minute!"

Leaving Constance standing dumbfounded at the top of the stairs, Edwin disappeared into the kitchen. "See you on Sunday, Mother," he shouted.

As he wheeled his bike from the garage and leant it up against the wall, he conceded to a small twinge of guilt over the way he'd dismissed his mother, but he quickly cast it aside and set his mind to the day ahead. Locking the garage door, he hopped on and pedalled off down the drive.

*

Descending the staircase on her stairlift, Constance was still reeling from Edwin's uncharacteristic display of insolence. "What sort of son leaves his poor, disabled mother to fend for herself?" she mumbled. When she reached the bottom of the staircase, she unclipped the safety belt on the chair and unsteadily got to her feet. "If his father could see the way he treats me he'd be appalled." Reaching for the walker, she paused for a moment, listening intently. "Edwin?" she called softly. There was no reply. Just to be sure, she called again, a little louder. Still no reply. Satisfied that he was gone, she disdainfully pushed the walker to one side. With only the faintest trace of difficulty, she sauntered unaided across the hall and through to the kitchen.

She crossed to the fridge, opened the door and looked inside. Unimpressed, she poked a bony finger at the stacked of ready meals inside. "Muck!" she exclaimed and angrily slammed the door shut.

*

Edwin reached the railway station in record time and mentally patted himself on the back as he realised the exertion hadn't actually rendered him breathless. Quite the opposite in fact; he felt exhilarated. He chained up his bike on the rack outside the entrance and, with a distinctly sprightly gait, went inside. He walked up to the ticket office and bought a ticket. Then, whistling loudly, he sprinted up the stairs and across the footbridge onto the platform and took a seat to await the arrival of the next train to Eastbourne.

CHAPTER 7

It was another sweltering hot day. At the St Joshua's Hospice Charity shop, Sylvia and Judy had been sorting clothing donations all morning. Fortunately it had been quiet in the shop – only a handful of customers had come in, the heat keeping people from venturing out unnecessarily, Judy surmised – and although there were still several large boxes to be checked through, the light at the end of the tunnel was in sight.

Sylvia stood upright with her hands on her hips. "I can hardly believe Beryl's 70 today," she said, wincing as the muscles in her lower back screamed at her.

"I know," Judy chuckled. "She's been with St Joshua's for almost five years now, you know."

"No!"

"Yes. She started volunteering two days after her 65th birthday, I remember it well."

Sylvia shook her head in disbelief. "Surely not! Five years?"

Judy inserted a hanger into a particularly attractive blouse and hung it on the rack. "Well, only three and a half here. She was with me in Hastings then she followed me here when I transferred."

"Unbelievable. Where does the time go?" Sylvia picked up a skirt and handed it to Judy. "I've been here nearly six years you know."

Judy laughed. "You get less for murdering someone these days."

Sylvia chuckled. "By the way, what's the plan for tonight's bash?"

"I thought we'd go to the White Hart."

"I've not been there. Is it nice?"

Judy nodded. "Me and Dave went for our anniversary a couple of months ago. The food was really good. There was a nice atmosphere in there and it was pretty quiet for a weeknight. Hopefully it will be tonight too, but I called last night and booked a table for 7 o'clock just in case."

Putting the skirt on a clothes hanger, Sylvia smiled. "I'm really looking forward to it. How many are coming?"

"Not as many as I'd like," Judy said with a sigh. "Everyone has such busy lives. There'll be just the five of us. If anyone wants food they can have it, or we can just do drinks." Fanning her face with her hand and making a little puffing sound, she walked over to the open shop door. "Mind if I close this? It's letting in more heat than air this morning."

"I was thinking that." Sylvia agreed.

Judy knocked out the wedge with her foot and closed the door.

The hour-long run down to Eastbourne passed unremarkably. Edwin had been alone in the carriage for the duration of the entire journey. Lost in his own little world, he had sat staring out of the window at the South Downs countryside as it flashed past, and was taken by surprise when the conductor's voice sounded over the tannoy announcing his destination as the next stop. He stood up, slipped on a pair of sunglasses and put his jacket over his shoulders. Catching sight of his reflection in the window, it delighted him to see, that wearing it in that manner gifted him a somewhat rakish appeal; the epitome of cool, he thought. Then he picked up his rucksack and made his way through the carriage to the exit.

*

It was early afternoon by the time Edwin eventually made his way onto the Grand Parade. His first task upon arriving in Eastbourne had been to seek out a reasonably priced B&B. He'd managed to locate something quite easily in Trinity Place that didn't stretch his budget too far. And although he'd balked slightly at having to pay the full bill up front – "Too many bloomin' moonlight flitters. You can take it or leave it," the surly landlord of The Golden Views had grumbled – rather than spend too much time searching for accommodation, he'd agreed and handed over the cash. The name of the establishment was either an attempt at irony, or else it was an almighty misnomer; the view from the window of the bedroom to which the landlord had escorted Edwin wasn't one that anyone in their right mind would describe as *golden*. But it was nevertheless salubrious enough for his purposes and probably as good as anything he'd be likely to find at such short notice.

Now, as he rounded the corner onto the Grand Parade he stopped and surveyed the rows of shops ahead. They stretched away from him as far as his eye could see. He turned and looked down the street in the opposite direction. Again, countless shops tailed away into the distance. Quietly cursing himself for having left his mobile phone back at the B&B, he slipped off his sunglasses and looked up at the frontage of the nearby bookshop. He frowned; no visible premises number. Making a decision – unbeknownst to him at that moment, the correct one – he put his sunglasses back on and proceeded to make his way up the street, which for this time of the morning was curiously devoid of shoppers.

As he neared the St Joshua's Hospice Charity shop, Judy – who'd been standing in the window struggling to dress a mannequin – stepped back off the low dais and back on to the shop floor.

Sylvia, obsessively separating clothes-hanger size cubes from a little tub beside the till, looked up. "All done?"

"Yes. Finally! I swear those mannequins head office sent us weren't modelled on anyone human, everything just hangs like sack cloth!"

Sylvia laughed as Judy walked over to the back room. "I'm just going to take a short break and have a coffee. And I need to ring Dave about something."

Sylvia grinned impishly. "Make sure you call the correct number!"

"Ha bloody Ha!"

As the words left her lips and she disappeared into the back room, Edwin arrived outside the shop. He looked up at the St Joshua's Hospice sign and adjusted his jacket. Taking a deep breath, he gingerly reached for the handle. At the last moment he paused as he felt a sickening sensation in his stomach. His confidence momentarily having deserted him, he stepped back, turned and walked away up the street. He'd find a coffee shop first. Yes, that would be best. A nice hot coffee. Steady his nerves. Then he'd go back.

But no more than a hundred yards up the street he stopped and turned back again. This was ridiculous. He hadn't come all this way to drink coffee. He looked at his reflection in the shop window in front of him and carefully patted at his Brylcreem'd hair. Then, his face etched with 'you can do this' resolve, he strode confidently back towards the shop.

CHAPTER 8

Sylvia was still arranging the size cubes when the door opened and Edwin stepped in to the shop. He stopped short just inside the door. Sylvia looked up and smiled politely. "Good afternoon."

"Hello there. What a beautiful day," Edwin replied cheerfully.

"It certainly is."

Edwin stood near the door for a moment, scanning the shop. There was no-one else in sight. Then his eyes settled upon a pile of jigsaw puzzles on a shelf in the corner.

Sylvia hadn't seen the man before and, even though she continued sorting the cubes, as secondary nature she kept half an eye on Edwin as he walked over to inspect the plenteous assortment of puzzles.

He pulled out each one, studied the image on the front of the box, then carefully replaced it. He glanced over at Sylvia a couple of times. Could this be the lady he'd spoken to on the phone? She was much older than he'd imagined from her voice. Their eyes met and he smiled at her politely, then looked back down at the picture of Blenheim Palace on the front of the box in his hand, staring at it without really seeing it.

Behind him, the shop door opened and Beryl appeared, puffing heavily and heavily laden with shopping bags.

"Here she is," Sylvia said. "The bonny birthday girl."

Edwin looked up and caught Beryl's eye. They smiled at each other. Surely *this* isn't her, Edwin thought, starting to feel a little concerned. The possibility that the charity shop might be staffed exclusively by elderly ladies had never actually entered his mind. But now, for the first time since he'd formulated his plan the previous morning at work, it occurred to him that coming here might just have been folly.

Beryl struggled over to the till and set down her bags. "Phew! Birthday shopping!" she exclaimed.

Sylvia peered over the till at the array of carrier bags on the floor. "It looks like you've bought up half of Eastbourne."

"You should try carrying it, my love. It *feels* like I've bought half of Eastbourne." Beryl chuckled. "Anyway, I won't stop. I was just passing so I thought I'd pop in and check what time we're meeting tonight."

"Seven-ish. Judy's booked a table for us at the White Hart."

"Lovely. And…" Beryl bent down and withdrew a small box from one of the bags. "…I wanted to drop off this." She placed the box on the counter. "Cream cakes."

Sylvia's eyes lit up. "Oooooo!"

"One for you and one for our Judy. I take it she's in?"

"She's out back."

Still making a show of examining the range of jigsaw puzzles stacked on the shelf, Edwin was listening intently to the conversation. He took some solace in the surety that neither of them *sounded* like the woman he'd come all this way to see. And obviously there would be more people staffing a shop as big as this than just two elderly ladies. There had to be someone else. Maybe this Judy they'd just mentioned was the one?

"Good," Beryl was saying. "I went with jammy cream slices. I know they're Judy's favourites. I assume she's coming tonight?"

From the back room, Judy called out, "Of course Judy's coming tonight. Judy arranged it!"

There was a sudden loud clatter from the corner of the shop as, in his excitement at recognising Judy's voice, Edwin dropped the jigsaw puzzle. Startled by the noise, Beryl spun round as the pieces scattered across the floor. Mortified, Edwin dropped to his knees. Looking suitably embarrassed, he started scooping up handfuls of the pieces, hurriedly shovelling them back into the box.

Beryl turned back rolling her eyes at Sylvia.

Sylvia called over, "Do you need a hand over there, sir?"

Edwin popped his head up from behind a display unit filled with bric-a-brac. "No, no," he said, evidently flustered. "I'm fine. Mr Butterfingers!" As he dipped back down out of sight his face darkened. Idiot! Double-damned idiot! His mother, had she been here, would have taken cruel pleasure in belittling him in front of the two women – and would probably have administered a clip round the back of his head into the bargain. And he'd have deserved it too. How could he have made such a spectacle of himself? Idiot, idiot, *idiot*!

"Well, I'd better lug this lot home," Beryl said, bending down and gathering up her carrier bags. "See you tonight."

Sylvia smiled. "You can count on it. I've been looking forward to it! Toodle-oo."

"Bye Judy." Beryl shouted.

"See you at 7," Judy called out from the back. "And don't be late!"

As Beryl left the shop, Edwin stood up, patting a loose strand of his hair back into place. He walked over to the counter and set down the jigsaw on the counter, readjusting the lid. "I suppose I'd better buy this one now," he said, slightly sheepishly.

Sylvia smiled. "You don't have to feel obliged to." She looked at the picture. "But it's a very nice one."

Composing himself, Edwin felt in his pocket for his wallet. "No, no, I'd like to purchase it," he said, adopting his carefully rehearsed charming persona. "How much is it?"

Sylvia turned the box to look for the price and the lid almost came off again. "Whoops!" she exclaimed. "I think I'd better put some tape on this for you." Edwin gave her an appreciative nod as she pulled a couple of strips of Sellotape from a roll holder on the counter and deftly sealed the box lid on either side. "A thousand pieces. That'll keep you busy."

"Oh, it's not for me," Edwin said. "It's for my Mother. She loves her jigsaws."

"Then hopefully she'll enjoy this one. That'll be £4.00 please."

His ice blue eyes gleaming, Edwin handed over a £10 note. "Let's call it ten, shall we?"

Sylvia beamed at him. It seemed the doubts she'd had about this man when he first came into the shop had been unfounded. "That's very kind of you, thank you, Sir."

As Sylvia put the money in the till, Edwin tucked his wallet back into his pocket and looked hopefully past her in the direction of the back room. But there was no sign of the lady whose mellifluous voice had spurred a hundred fantasies in Edwin's head over the past two days.

Sylvia slid the puzzle into a bag emblazoned with the St Joshua's Hospice emblem and handed it to Edwin. "There you go."

"Thank you." Edwin smiled at her.

"Have a good day."

Edwin walked over to the door and loitered for a moment in a last ditch hope of setting eyes on the elusive Judy.

Again, that sixth sense sensation, Sylvia thought. "You alright there, sir?"

Edwin looked a little awkward and reached for the door handle. "I, er... no. Er... I mean yes. I'm fine. Thank you. Goodbye." With a last quick glance in the direction of the back room, Edwin walked out.

As the door swung shut behind him, Judy emerged from the back room. "What was all the racket about just now?"

"A customer dropped one of the jigsaw puzzles."

"I hope he bought it."

"He certainly did." Sylvia chuckled. "He paid more than double for it. He was clearly embarrassed that he'd dropped it. He was very sweet though. He bought it for his mother."

Judy smiled approvingly. "We could do with a few more customers like that." She walked across the shop. "Most of them haggle over 50 pence!" Bending down beside the display unit, she picked up a piece of jigsaw puzzle. "Oh no! He's left a bit behind," she said. "Was he one of the regulars?"

"No, I've not seen him before. But I'll tell you what… he had the most beautiful blue eyes." A dreamy look appeared on her face. "He reminded me of a young Frank Sinatra."

Judy returned to the counter. "Calm down, Mrs Bassett." She put the rogue piece of jigsaw down beside the till. "I'll leave it here just in case he comes back in."

*

Having enjoyed an hour or two exploring the promenade, which had given him ample time to ponder his next move, Edwin had arrived back at The Golden Views B&B a little before 4 o'clock. A big night lay ahead and he'd decided that getting his head down for an hour or so would be most beneficial.

Now he was seated on the edge of the bed, gazing at the charity shop bag. With a hint of elation on his face, he lightly traced his fingers around the shape of the St Joshua's Hospice emblem and smiled warmly. "Judy…" he murmured softly.

He laid down the bag on the bed beside him, got up and switched on an electric kettle on the table beside the bed. Pulling his phone from his rucksack, he accessed Google and tapped a few words into the search field. He looked at the result: A photograph of the exterior of The White Hart Inn, Eastbourne. Below the photograph there was an address. He scribbled it down and smiled.

The kettle boiled and he prepared himself a cup of weak tea. He surveyed The Golden Views' meagre assortment of courtesy biscuits that had been neatly arranged on a tray beside the kettle. He scowled at the Garibaldis. Dead fly biscuits, his mother had called them, cackling with amusement as she'd forced him to eat one. The childhood incident, as silly as he now realised it had been, has nevertheless left him with a deep-rooted dislike of the hideous things. Dislike? No, it was *more* than that. He absolutely despised them and felt his gorge rising just looking at them.

Tossing the offending packet into the wastebasket, he selected a duo-pack of custard creams from what little choice remained. He stretched out on the bed with his head propped up on the pillow. Looking very pleased with himself, he took a small sip of the steaming tea, dunked one of the custard creams into the cup and popped it whole into his mouth.

CHAPTER 9

Not that Edwin had an awful lot to gauge it by –
social drinking wasn't really his thing – but in his
estimation The White Hart Inn wasn't the most
welcoming pub in which to spend an evening.
Unless, of course, you happened to like football, in
which case you'd think you'd found nirvana. The
walls were bedecked with framed photographs of
local teams, some of them dating back decades.

Edwin sat staring up at the faded picture on
the wall above his corner booth: 'Eastbourne
Athletic, 1922' the caption beneath the photo stated.
Edwin disliked football with a passion. He'd never
understood how people could get so excited watching
22 grown men kick a piece of leather around a field.
His disdain, as with many things for Edwin, was born
of childhood experience. Passion begot passion in his
opinion and those who were keen on sports usually
had fathers who had passed on that passion. Edwin's
father hadn't been sporty at all and gave the game –
and those who raved on about it – short shrift.
Subsequently, simply through absence of exposure to
the Saturday afternoon match or whatever, Edwin had
never cultivated an interest in it either. In adult life it
seldom, if ever posed a problem, but at school he'd
immediately become a pariah. Those humilating
selections when the captains – the best players –

worked along the line-up of kids, alternately picking a member for their team, had been living nightmares for Edwin. He was always one of the last two, at whichpoint he was reluctantly selected over Ian Warren, the bespectacled kid with a limp. It hadn't helped either that Mr Jones, the sports teacher took a swift dislike to him. Sports teacher? Sports bully, more like. In his head, Edwin could still hear the man hollering at him as he reluctantly stood in defence, shivering with the cold, on the rain-lashed pitch: "Come on, Edwina, you big girl's blouse! Get stuck in there, lad!"

Edwin shook off the memory and surveyed his surroundings. One thing The White Hart did have going for it was that it was very quiet. There were two men standing at the bar talking and drinking lager, and an elderly man seated on his own at a table near the door nursing a pint of Guinness. And, of course, there was the St Joshua's Hospice Charity group's birthday celebration.

Edwin had purposely chosen his position in the room to provide him with the best possible vantage point for surveillance. The group were seated at a small table on the far side of the bar. From where Edwin sat, he had a clear view of Sylvia and Beryl – between whom there was an ostentatious foil helium balloon in the shape of a cartoonish number 70 gently bobbing on a string – but, frustratingly, Judy had taken a seat with her back to him and as of now he'd still not managed to see her face.

Also seated with them was Brenda Keeley, another of the volunteers from the charity shop. Beryl had a few little gift bags on the floor beside her chair and she stood up laughing hysterically, holding up in front of her an apron emblazoned with a crude depiction of a naked lady.

It had only just turned 7.30, but the atmosphere was already very convivial. As Edwin watched, sipping on an orange juice and lemonade and peering at the group from behind a table menu, Terry Mardell the shops delivery driver stepped over from the bar with a tray of drinks. Pushing aside the collection of drained glasses on the table, he just about managed to make room for the fresh libation, then gathered up the empties and nipped back over to the bar to return the tray.

"It's a real shame some of the others couldn't make it," Sylvia remarked as she picked up her vodka tonic and took a sip.

Beryl folded the apron and dropped it into one of the bags, emptied her glass of red wine and picked up the fresh one. "Not to worry," she said. "This is very nice, just the five of us." She smiled over at Judy gratefully. "Thank you so much for organising it, love."

Terry reappeared and took a seat. "Everyone sorted?" Amidst a small hubbub of thank-yous, he looked at the table and exclaimed, "Bloomin' 'eck, I've only gone and forgotten my own!" The women all burst out laughing.

As Terry returned to the bar, Beryl called out "Oh, can you see if they've got any peanuts, love? Salted type, not the dry roast, they play havoc with my insides."

Sylvia laughed.

Beryl looked indignant. "Well they do. They give me awful wind."

Judy stood up. "On that note, I'm just going to powder my nose."

At precisely the same moment, the rotund woman who'd served Edwin at the bar upon his arrival – and put ice in his drink, despite his specific request to have it without – stepped over and stopped directly in front of him. Her bulk completely obscured his view of the group. "Alright there, my love? Are you ready to order?"

Edwin made a slightly exasperated sound and tried to peer around the fulsome woman, but she was having none of it. "Food?" she said.

Edwin quickly scanned the menu as the woman looked down at him. "I know there's a lot to choose from, but you've been staring the type off it for the last ten minutes. I thought you might have decided by now." Her jovial tone failed to disguise a hint of impatience. "I can come back…"

Edwin glanced at the section on the menu headed up Light Snacks. He just wanted this annoying woman to go away. "No, no," he mumbled. "Er…I'll have a cheese jacket with a salad please."

"That everything, sir?"

Edwin leaned over in another attempt to see around her and, as he realised Judy was no longer anywhere to be seen, his face filled with mild panic.

The woman looked around to see what was distracting him and then, rather tersely, repeated the question. "Is that *everything*?"

"Oh, yes, that's all," Edwin said, slightly apologetically.

"Be about ten minutes." The woman turned and walked away.

His eyes scanning the room, Edwin drained the last of his orange juice and lemonade, stood up and crossed to the bar.

The barman placed two fresh glasses of lager down on the counter in front of the two men and looked up over at Edwin enquiringly. "Yes, sir?"

"Orange juice and lemonade please. And no ice this time."

The barman nodded. "Coming right up."

As Edwin leant on the bar waiting for his drink, raucous laughter sounded from the corner and he turned his head to look at them.

The barman placed the drink in front of him. "That'll be £3.50, please sir."

Edwin paid and turned to go back to the booth, but just as he did so, Judy appeared right behind him on her way back from the ladies' room to her table. Edwin just managed to keep hold of his glass as she collided with him, but some of the content splashed out over his hand and across the sleeve of his brand new jacket.

Judy looked horrified. "Oh, my God, I'm *so* terribly sorry!"

Frowning, Edwin looked at her and his expression of annoyance melted away. His ice blue eyes almost sparkled as he finally set eyes on the very woman he'd come to see. For a moment he was lost for words, then with spilt juice dripping off his hand, he set down his glass on the bar.

"That's perfectly okay, no harm done."

Judy hastily pulled out a handkerchief from her handbag and passed it to him. "Here, use this. And let me buy you another drink."

Edwin smiled appreciatively, took the handkerchief from her and dabbed at his hand. "Not necessary. Just a tiny spill." He looked over at Judy's friends. "Someone's birthday?"

Judy was momentarily confused.

"The balloon," he continued.

"Oh!" Judy laughed. "Yes, it's my friend, she's 70 today."

Edwin handed the damp handkerchief back to her. She glanced at the sodden square of material. "No, please, you can keep it," she said hastily. "So sorry, I hope it washes out."

"Please," Edwin said, "you've nothing to apologise for."

A vague look of recognition at his words crossed Judy's face, but the moment passed as her colleagues burst out laughing.

Edwin smiled at her. "Better let you get back to the party."

"Yes. Well, sorry again."

Edwin returned to his corner booth and Judy walked back over to join her friends. As she sat down she noticed Beryl grinning at her broadly. "What?"

Beryl chuckled. "You're incorrigible, you. We can't take you anywhere!"

Judy pursed her lips. "What are you on about now?"

Beryl took a sip of her wine. "Well..." she said, teasingly. "If you're not chatting up strangers on the phone, you're accosting innocent men in pubs."

Judy rolled her eyes. "You're not gonna let that stupid call drop, are you?"

Beryl smiled at her sweetly. "Nope," she said chirpily. "Do I ever let anything drop?"

Terry raised his eyebrows. "Chatting up strangers? This sounds interesting."

"It really *isn't*," Judy sighed.

Brenda laughed. "Are you stirring again, Beryl Foster?"

Beryl gave her an innocent 'who, me?' look.

"That's *exactly* what she's doing," Judy said casting a disapproving look across the table.

Sylvia, who'd been squinting across at Edwin, suddenly said, "Hey, isn't that the guy who dropped the puzzle in the shop this afternoon?"

Beryl looked and shook her head. "I don't know. I didn't pay that much attention." A mischievous twinkle appeared in her eye. "Why don't you go over and ask him, Judy?"

Judy, who had just taken a mouthful of her rum and coke, almost spat it out. "*What*?! Why me?" she spluttered.

"Well, you're obviously already the best of mates with him."

"What *are* you…"

"Making google eyes at him while you were at the bar." Beryl grinned.

Judy looked at her incredulously. "Don't be so ridic…"

"Plus you *are* the boss," Beryl added.

Judy shook her head. You're the boss: the definitive answer to everything. She set down her drink on the table. "Okay, if it'll shut you up, I'll go over and ask him."

Edwin was seated at his table admiring the handkerchief – *her* handkerchief – as Judy stood up. He delicately ran it through his hands and between his fingers, revelling in how it made him feel. The texture of the soft, damp cloth made him tingle deep down inside. It was a little piece of Judy. She'd touched it. She'd *given* it to him. And now it was his.

Out of the corner of his eye he caught a movement and, looking up, realised Judy was walking towards him. Surely she wasn't going to ask for it back! He hastily tucked the sodden handkerchief into his jacket pocket. Patting at his hair over each ear, he stood up to greet her.

Judy smiled at him. "Hi, sorry to disturb you – again. But did you purchase a jigsaw puzzle from a charity shop on the Grand Parade this afternoon?"

The question momentarily threw him. "Er, yes, indeed I did."

"I understand you inadvertently showered the floor with it." Judy laughed.

Edwin looked a little sheepish. "Oh, er… yes, I did. Clumsy oaf, eh?"

Judy realised she'd embarrassed him, which hadn't been her intention at all. "No," she said quickly, "they really should be taped up. The thing is, after you left we found a piece on the floor."

"Oh!" Edwin looked relieved. "And it was bound to be most important bit too." Judy laughed. Such an enchanting laugh. The sound was music to Edwin's ears.

"Isn't it always?" she said. "Anyway, I put it aside for you by the till and next time you're in town just pop in and pick it up."

"How very kind of you. I shall certainly do so. Tomorrow perhaps? May I ask if you'll be there?"

Judy smiled. "I shall. And there'll be no extra charge."

Edwin stood smiling at her. Beautiful *and* a sense of humour. Judy was turning out to be more perfect than he could possibly have hoped for, everything he'd imagined and so much more besides.

The idyllic moment was abruptly shattered as the portly woman who'd taken Edwin's order appeared with his food. Rudely stepping between the two of them, she set the plate down on the table. "One cheese jacket and side salad, sir. Anything else I can get you? Sauces? Condiments?"

Edwin frowned slightly, annoyed at the intrusion. "No, that's fine, thank you."

The woman turned and walked away.

Judy seized upon the opportunity to return to her own table. "Well, I'll leave you in peace to enjoy your meal."

As she started to turn away, Edwin extended his hand. "Until tomorrow?" There was a pregnant pause. Judy looked at him standing there with his hand held out expectantly.

"Oh, yes, er… sorry." Judy reached out and warmly shook his hand. Edwin felt the blood rush through him, his face suddenly felt warm and for an instant he thought his heart was going to explode. "Nice to have met you," Judy continued. "Goodbye."

Edwin stood watching her as she gracefully walked back over to her table. He sat down and put his hand to his face.

He could smell her perfume on his fingers. It was the most wonderful thing he'd ever smelt in his life and he made a mental note to try to find out what it was when he got back home.

He looked up as raucous laughter resounded from the other side of the room. Were they laughing at his expense? He actually didn't care. At that moment he was floating among the clouds.

He looked up at the photograph of Eastbourne Athletic. The faces of the eleven, long since dead footballers smiled down at him. All of a sudden, to Edwin, the White Hart's décor didn't seem quite so bad after all. Raising his glass to the picture, he took a sip, and then dug into his meal with gusto.

*

At precisely the same moment that Edwin was busy falling in love, Constance was standing at the kitchen table struggling to open one of the microwave ready meals he'd purchased for her.

She'd managed to get the lasagne out of the carton – although why they provided 'pull here' tabs that didn't actually work was completely beyond her – and now her fingers were shaking and she endeavoured to peel the cellophane seal off the tray. Eventually managing to remove it in three strips, she picked up the carton to inspect the cooking instructions. Her eyes widened in anger as she realised she was supposed to have pierced the cellophane and not removed it until *after* cooking.

In a fit of pique, she tossed the tray to the floor and lasagne splattered across the tiles and up the wall. "Wherever you are, I hope you're having a perfectly horrible time, you ungrateful, selfish boy!"

She took a packet of bourbon biscuits from the cupboard and poured a glass of milk. She shuffled back into the living room mumbling to herself as she went and took up her favorite position behind a jigsaw puzzle.

CHAPTER 10

The following morning, Edwin was up with the lark. Still reeling with delight over his meeting with Judy the previous evening, at 8 o'clock on the dot he went downstairs and took a seat alone in The Golden Views' tiny dining room. With the aid of two large mugs of tea, he wolfed down a grease-drenched breakfast comprising sausage, bacon, scrambled egg, mushrooms and fried bread. He didn't even care for mushrooms, but such was his mood that he ate them anyway. More charitably, he didn't even consider contesting the landlord's patently fraudulent claim that this was 'The finest cooked breakfast you would ever find outside of the Savoy'. It had crossed his mind that there was probably a long haul truckers' café called the Savoy in Bexhill or Pevensey Bay and the thought made him smile.

The landlord, who'd just arrived clutching a teapot, noticed the expression on Edwin's face. "You enjoyed it then?" he said with an evident note of satisfaction.

"Hmmm," Edwin replied noncommittally.

"Told ya!" He pointed to the tannin stained blue and white teapot. "Another?"

Edwin held up a hand. "No thank you."

"Yeah," the man continued enthusiastically. "That posh London crowd could learn a thing or two from my cooking, I tell ya. And – Mine doesn't cost a king's ransom either!"

So he *had* meant the Savoy in London. This amused Edwin even more. He smiled up at his host. "I'm in no doubt at all that they could," he replied, trying not to sound sarcastic.

The landlord might have detected a trace of irony, but if he had then he chose to ignore it. He winked, whipped up Edwin's empty plate and disappeared out to the kitchen.

*

There were a couple of customers – a husband and wife – mooching around in the St Joshua's Hospice Charity shop; the sort that browse for ages, looking for nothing in particular and then leave without actually buying anything. That said, Beryl noticed the wife had spent an inordinate amount of time looking at their rack of greetings cards – and now had two clutched in her hand – and she readily stepped over to the till just in case. Sylvia, meanwhile, was seated on a low stool with a pile of jigsaw puzzle boxes in front of her, carefully applying Sellotape to each of them.

The radio was on low, and a bouncy Herman's Hermit's song was playing. The two women were singing along, one alternate line each; song tennis, Beryl called it.

Beryl was just about managing to carry the tune: "She danced close to me like I hoped she would…" she warbled, pointing at Sylvia.

"Something tells me I'm into something good!" Sylvia batted back, completely out of tune.

Beryl chuckled. "Who let the cat out?" The smile dropped from her face as she noticed the woman returning the greetings cards to the rack. So, she thought, they *were* those sort of customers after all – Timewasters! She watched as the couple made to leave, almost colliding in the doorway with a man on his way in.

Edwin stood back to let the couple pass, then came in to the shop. Patting at his Brylcreem'd hair to ensure it was perfectly in place, he walked straight over towards the till.

Beryl smiled at him. "Good morning. How can I help you?"

"Hello!" Edwin exclaimed cheerfully. "I've come to pick up my missing jigsaw piece."

Beryl looked at him, momentarily confused. "Your missing…?" Then the penny dropped. "Oh, yes, the jigsaw piece. Of course." She began to ferret around amongst the till-side clutter, but she couldn't find it. She smiled sweetly at Edwin and he smiled back. "Just one moment." She turned in the direction of the back room and shouted, "Judy, the gentleman has come in for his jigsaw piece. Where did you put it love?"

"It's by the till," Judy's voice called out.

Beryl turned her attention back to Edwin. "Sorry, won't keep you a moment."

Edwin beamed. "It's fine, I'm not in a hurry to be anywhere."

Beryl took another look around the till, then shouted, "I can't see it!"

As Judy appeared from the back room and her eyes met Edwin's, his mouth broadened into a winning smile.

"Hello again," Judy said cheerfully. She crossed to the till and leant across Beryl, inadvertently affording Edwin a tantalising glimpse of her cleavage. In a gentlemanly fashion he averted his eyes and pretended to be surveying the shop. She located the piece of puzzle and slid it across the counter towards Edwin. "There you go, sir."

Edwin smiled at her. "Thank you. I must say, this is a wonderful shop you have here. A real treasure trove." He turned away and waved a hand in the air. "One could spend hours delving into its hidden delights."

Unnoticed by Edwin, Beryl subtly raised her eyebrows at Judy.

Judy broke into her standard patter. "We always have a great selection of donated items at really good prices."

Edwin turned to face her. " I can see that."

"We operate in aid of life limited local children," Judy continued. "And we're non-profit.

All the proceeds go directly to giving them a better quality of life."

Edwin fumbled in his pocket. "Listen. You've been so kind, I'd like to make a donation." He withdrew his wallet and pulled out several crisp, new £20 notes.

Judy's eyes widened. "That's very kind of you," she said, pointing to a collection tin on the counter. "Just pop it in there."

Edwin folded the notes and attempted to slip them into the slot on the tin, but the generous wodge wouldn't fit. "Ah!" he exclaimed, hesitating as if he wasn't sure what to do next. Come on, Edwin, he thought, don't make a fool of yourself again. "Well," he said, handing the neatly folded notes to Beryl, "here you are."

Beryl smiled gratefully and passed them to Judy. Without unfolding the bundle, Judy estimated there was at least £80 there. She gasped. "Thanks *so* much. That's very, very kind of you, Sir!"

Edwin chuckled with pleasure. "No, really, thank *you*. And please, call me Ed." He carefully tucked the piece of puzzle into his wallet. "I'll reunite this with its siblings later on."

Judy laughed. That heavenly sound again, Edwin thought. "Most expensive piece of jigsaw puzzle I've ever bought, mind you," he said. "All for a worthy cause though."

Judy nodded appreciatively. "Maybe we'll see you again sometime?"

"You can count on it," Edwin replied enthusiastically. "Well, goodbye for now."

As he turned to leave, Sylvia – who had been watching Edwin since he'd walked in – stepped over and picked up a small magazine from a pile on the counter. "Oh, Sir. Here, please take one of our monthly magazines."

Edwin took the magazine from her and his blue eyes lit up. There, smiling out at him from the front cover was Judy.

"Oh!" he exclaimed with delight. "Look!" He gazed over at Judy and pointed at the cover. "It's you!"

Judy's cheeks flushed with embarrassment. "Yeah... Don't ask!"

"St Joshua's regional shop manager of the year," Sylvia said proudly.

"For the second year running," added Beryl.

Edwin chuckled. "It's an absolutely delightful picture." He smiled at Judy warmly.

Through a blush, she smiled back. "Thank you."

Edwin nodded. "Thank *you*. Well, I must be off." Then he turned on his heels, crossed smartly to the doorway and, without looking back, walked out.

Beryl and Sylvia looked at each other; an unspoken 'Aww, isn't he sweet?' passed between the two of them.

Beryl began to open her mouth, but Judy cut her short: "Don't you say a word!"

The ladies returned to their work in silence.

CHAPTER 11

After he left the shop, Edwin decided he'd take a walk. Following a brief stop to inspect the Wish Tower and admire the view back across the bay from the hilltop upon which it had stood since the early 1800s, he took himself up to the cliffs at Beachy Head. He'd not been to Eastbourne for many years and one of his fondest memories – and there weren't too many of those – was of a picnic with his grandmother on the cliff top overlooking the sea.

It didn't take him as long as he expected to get there despite the steep climb and as soon as he arrived, the memories came flooding back. Although the little cafeteria where his grandmother had bought him a strawberry ice cream looked much smaller than he remembered, he was delighted to see it was still there and it was open for business.

The elderly woman who served him at the outside window apologised profusely for having run out of strawberry, so he opted instead for a plain 99. He then spent a couple of pleasant hours strolling along the cliff top, formulating his plan for the following morning and thinking about how his life was finally taking an upturn.

*

Sylvia was busy mopping up the pool of blackcurrant juice carelessly deposited on the floor by the irksome little brat whose mother had refused to buy him a Spider-Man toy and had to haul him kicking and screaming out of the shop, apologising profusely for her son's petulant behaviour.

Beryl thanked a customer who'd just purchased three paperback novels and a DVD, waiting for him to leave before going out to the back room. "Is it okay if I nip out to get myself a bit of lunch?" she asked Judy.

Judy, down on her knees, stopped sifting through the box of assorted bric-a-brac in front of her. "Sure." With a little groaning noise and briskly rubbing at her knees, she got to her feet.

"Want anything yourself?" Beryl asked, collecting her purse from her handbag.

Judy shook her head. "No thanks." She accompanied Beryl back out onto the shop floor where Sylvia had just finished mopping up. "Can you watch the till while Beryl's out please?".

Sylvia nodded. "Of course."

"Get you anything, Sylv?"

"Ooo, yes please. I've had a hankering for a prawn and mayo sandwich all morning. Hang on and I'll get you the money."

"Pay me later," Beryl said, as she crossed to the door. "Nothing else?"

Sylvia reached round the door into the back room and leant the mop against the wall. "No, just the prawn and mayo." She looked at Judy. "I still can't believe how much that guy gave us this morning."

"I know," Judy said. "He can come in as often as he likes."

Beryl paused in the open doorway, her hearing remarkably good for someone of her years. She laughed out loud. "See?" she said mischievously. "Absolutely incorrigible!"

Judy pointed at her. "Oi you! I already told you, don't start! You know *exactly* what I meant."

*

Lost in his own little world, Edwin had walked much further along the cliffs than he'd intended and the return hike had taken it out of him. Stopping at a confectioner's to make a purchase, he'd returned to The Golden Views and decided to take a late afternoon siesta. Now he awoke with a start and realised he'd slept for 3 hours. Resigning himself to the fact he simply wasn't as young as he used to be, he got up and changed into a pair of striped pyjamas, neatly folded up his clothes and placed them on the table alongside the jigsaw puzzle of Blenheim Palace and a large box of handmade chocolates.

He picked up his phone, sat on the edge of the bed and scrolled to the number identified on the screen as 'Home'.

Constance was sitting in her armchair working on her jigsaw puzzle when the phone rang. Lifting a small plate of half chewed crusts of bread from the arm of the chair, she placed it on top of the puzzle. She got to her feet and unhurriedly made her way across the room. "I'm coming, I'm coming," she mumbled testily. She went out into the hall and approached the wall-mounted telephone, but just as she reached for the receiver the ringing stopped. She screwed up her face.

Edwin stared at his phone and frowned. Why wasn't she answering? His successful day had instilled in him a rare touch of compassion for his mother, which is why he'd decided to check in on her. Now he felt annoyed and almost couldn't be bothered to try again, but then thought better of it. He tapped in the number a second time.

Constance had just stepped back into the sitting room when the phone started ringing again. "Oh botheration!" she exclaimed and, putting an arm on the door frame to steady herself, turned round. She crossed to the phone and lifted the receiver. "Hello?" she said impatiently.

"Hello? Is that you, Mother?"

A look of abject disdain crossed Constance's face. "Who's that?"

Edwin flinched. "Who's *that*? How many people call you Mother? It's me. Edwin."

Constance adopted a slightly hurt tone. "Oh, it's *you*. Finally remembered that you've *got* a mother then?"

"Oh don't be silly," Edwin replied. Why did she always have to try to make him feel so small? "Of course I know I have a mother. I was worried there for a moment when you didn't answer."

Constance looked over at her walker, sitting at the bottom of the stairs where it had been parked unemployed since the previous morning. She afforded herself a sly smile. "You know I struggle with that useless walker. It takes me time to get from my chair to the phone. It caught on the door frame."

"I know, I'm sorry."

"Well, what do you want, boy?"

I just wanted to check everything's alright there, that's all."

"Of course everything's alright," Constance snapped. "I'm perfectly capable of looking after myself, you know!"

Edwin shook his head in disbelief. "That's good then. You're eating properly?"

Constance said indignantly, "I am, thank you very much. And not any of that inedible rubbish you filled the fridge with."

Edwin sighed. There was little mileage in continuing the conversation. "Okay, well I'll be home day after tomorrow. Is there anything we need?"

Constance scowled. "As if you give two hoots about what *I* might need. If you did you wouldn't have gone off gallivanting off in the first place would you?!"

"Very well, Mother. I'll see you on Sunday. Goodbye." Edwin tapped the screen to end the call.

Constance stood holding the receiver, listening to the quiet purring sound of a disconnected line. "Hello?... Hello?... Are you still there, boy??" Getting no reply, she angrily slammed the receiver back into its cradle.

Edwin finished folding his clothing. Then, patting at his hair, he reached over to his jacket and retrieved the rolled up charity shop magazine. Judy smiled up at him from the cover.

He bent down and fished out a Swiss Army knife from the side pocket on his rucksack. It had been a 12th birthday present from his grandmother – she'd died just two weeks later and he'd been heartbroken – and although he was well aware that carrying a knife around was illegal, it went everywhere with him. Opening the tiny scissors, he carefully cut the cover off the magazine and deposited the remains in the wastebasket. He crossed to the bed and placed the picture on the pillow, then climbed in under the blanket and rested his head beside it. My word, she's beautiful, he thought.

"Goodnight," he whispered softly. Planting a gentle kiss on her cheek, he reached over and switched off the bedside lamp.

CHAPTER 12

At 9 o'clock the following morning, Edwin stepped out of the front door of The Golden Views with the box of chocolates lovingly tucked under his arm and a discernible spring in his step. The landlord was just coming through the gate carrying a large box with the word 'fragile' stencilled on the side. He set it down on the ground and stepped aside to let Edwin pass. "You're looking very dapper this morning, if I may say so, sir."

Edwin beamed. "Thank you. Just off out to meet a friend."

The landlord picked up the box and paused to watch Edwin stride purposefully off up the street. He smiled. "Nice man."

As Edwin reached the end of Hartlington Place, he spotted a florists shop across the road on the corner of Compton Street. He crossed over and, after a quick glance at the display in the window, went inside. Five minutes later he emerged carrying a bunch of white roses and made his way down to the Grand Parade. To the casual observer he might have appeared perfectly relaxed, but inside his stomach was doing cartwheels and his mind was racing.

When he got to the St Joshua's shop door, he stopped and peered through the glass. To his delight, except for one customer, Judy was alone in the shop. He patted at his perfectly Brylcreem'd coiffeur and drew a deep breath. He'd rehearsed this moment in his head a hundred times and now the time had come. Don't mess it up, Colthorpe, he thought as he pushed open the door.

The customer was just finishing her purchase at the till. Edwin paused and held the door open for her; she smiled and nodded appreciatively as she walked past. Edwin let the door swing shut.

Judy smiled at him. "Hello there."

Edwin almost swooned at the sight of her and for a moment he thought he was actually going to pass out on the spot.

Judy's eyes fell on the bunch of flowers in his hand. Feigning an expression of surprise, she put her hand to her chest. "Oh you shouldn't have."

Edwin crossed to the counter and adopted a winning smile. "Beautiful flowers for a beautiful lady," he said, handing the roses to her.

Judy looked rather taken aback. "Oh! I was joking! Really?" She didn't know what to say. "You were more than generous to the shop yesterday."

Edwin shook his head with amusement. "You misunderstand. These are not for the shop. They're for you, Judy. As are these…" His ice blue eyes sparkled as he set the box of chocolates down on the counter in front of her.

Judy looked at him questioningly. How did he know her name?

Edwin saw the expression on her face and immediately realised he'd overstepped the mark. "I do apologise," he said hastily. "That was very presumptuous of me. I heard your colleague call you Judy, and I…"

Judy smiled at him warmly. "Oh no, It's fine. You can call me Judy." She laughed. "It is my name after all."

Edwin smiled back at her and nodded. "Thank you, Judy."

"Well, look," Judy began. "Thank you, you're very kind, but it really wasn't necessary. It was only a missing jigsaw piece."

"The jigsaw piece?" Edwin beamed. "That just proved what a kind and thoughtful person you really are."

Judy looked a little embarrassed. "Well, that's a nice thing to say. So, er… thank you again then. The flowers are lovely and I'll share the chocolates with my colleagues."

Edwin shook his head. "No, you don't understand, they're yours. I bought them for you."

Judy looked at him, slightly confused. Where was this leading?

Edwin took a deep breath and cleared his throat. "Look, this is a little bit awkward, so I think I'll just come straight out and say it. I was wondering if you would you do me the very great honour of accompanying me out for dinner this evening?"

Judy looked taken aback. If she'd had been given five guesses as to what Edwin was going to say next, this wouldn't have been one of them. Momentarily lost for words, she stared at him in silence. It was only a matter of seconds before she spoke, but to Edwin – who stood looking at her with an expectant smile on his face – it felt like an eternity. "I don't know what to say," she stammered.

Edwin's eyes twinkled. "You say yes," he said. "I've seen that there are some rather splendid looking restaurants here in Eastbourne. You could choose which one you'd like to try," he said, hoping to sweeten the invite. "And naturally," he added, "it will be my treat."

Judy had to force a smile. "That's ever so sweet of you. And I'd love to come, but…"

"Then say yes," Edwin cut in.

"I'd *love* to come," Judy repeated. "Really I would. But you see, the thing is…well, I'm married."

When she reflected on the moment later, Judy would only have been able to describe Edwin's reaction as that of a child who'd just been told his beloved pet had died. The amicable smile vanished, the light in his blue eyes went out and the colour drained from his face. He stood staring at her blankly.

"Sorry," Judy said apologetically, for no other reason than to break the horrible silence.

Though clearly crestfallen Edwin appeared to compose himself. He forced a smile. "It's me who should be apologising."

"You've nothing to apologise for." Judy put a hand to her chest. "I'm touched. Really I am. But I just can't."

Edwin began to shuffle awkwardly away from the counter, bumping into a display unit. "No," he insisted. "I've made a ridiculous fool of myself. Please accept my most humble apologies." He turned and hurried to the door.

Judy called, "Please, don't be upset. I…"

As he went to leave, Edwin turned and looked back at her, an indefinable expression on his face. His eyes were moist with tears. "Goodbye," he said politely.

The door swung shut behind him, leaving Judy standing at the counter dumbfounded.

Beryl's face appeared around the door of the back room and she spotted the flowers and chocolates on the counter. "Oooo," she cooed. "Late birthday present *pour moi*?" She saw the look on Judy's face and her smile faded. She came out onto the shop floor. "You alright, love?"

Judy picked up the flowers and the chocolates. "Watch the till, would you?" She walked past Beryl in silence and disappeared into the back room.

Beryl hesitated and would have followed Judy in, but at that moment the shop door opened and two women, chattering away to each other, came in. She stepped over to the till. "Good morning."

Her mind racing, Judy laid Edwin's gifts on the table and sat down. What on earth had just happened? She barely even knew this guy. Had she inadvertently done something to encourage him? No, she hadn't. Of that she was certain. But the look of hurt on his face when she'd told him she was married had cut right through her. And his expression when he'd looked back at her from the doorway. His eyes had been filled with sadness, like... like a dying animal. No, that wasn't quite right. The more Judy thought about it, the more Edwin's expression spurred a memory of the look on her boyfriend Andy Pearson's face as she'd jilted him on the night of the end of term disco. Yes, that was it, she thought: sadness, for sure, but there had been a hint of menace buried in there too.

Beside her on the table a computer screen was showing a CCTV image of the shop floor. Judy stared blankly at the screen, seeing it, yet not seeing it. Two women were at the counter talking to Beryl. A movement top left of the screen caught her eye. The picture wasn't that clear, but she could clearly make out the shape of a man standing outside the shop window looking in. Was it him?

Judy jumped to her feet, wrenched open the door and stared across towards the shop window. The elderly man who'd stopped to take a breather and bent forward to examine the display of wristwatches through the glass, stood upright. As he did so, he caught sight of Judy staring at him from inside the shop. He nodded at her politely, then turned and slowly walked away.

*

Everything Edwin had been hoping for had turned to mush and he couldn't put the shop and that horrible moment of embarrassment behind him fast enough. He'd been half way up the street before he'd realised he was going in the wrong direction.

He stopped and spun round to get his bearings. What were his options? There was no way he was going to walk back past the shop. Maybe there was a side street further along the Grand Parade he could take and then circle back round. Deciding to do that, he took off abruptly, almost knocking an elderly lady off her feet. He mumbled an apology and – ignoring the woman's angry protestations that he should look where he's going – continued on without even looking back.

Beyond the fact it seemed to take him forever, Edwin would later remember little of his return to The Golden Views. Breathing heavily, he took the stairs two at a time, burst into his room and slammed the door shut behind him. He grabbed his rucksack from the floor and flung his neatly folded clothing roughshod into it. He angrily snatched up the magazine cover from the bedside table and was about to hurl it into the waste paper basket when he stopped. Holding it aloft, he smoothed the creases.

He looked at Judy's pretty face smiling out at him and his anger drained as if someone had suddenly thrown an off switch.

He sighed loudly and slumped down on the end of the bed. Clutching the picture in both hands and with a thick curl of loose hair flopping across his eyes, he stared down at it. There'd been a connection between them; he'd felt it, she must have felt it too. He had rehearsed the scenario in his head over and over. It had been perfect. How could she have turned him down so coldly? *How*?

A solitary tear rolled down his cheek and dripped onto the picture.

CHAPTER 13

Three hours later Edwin emerged from the entrance of Rye station with his rucksack slung over his shoulder. His shoulders hunched and a forlorn expression on his face, he walked over to the bike rack and stopped short at the sight in front of him.

There were two bikes parked in the rack; a ladies bike with a shopping basket on the front and, beside it, the twisted remains of Edwin's. The saddle was missing, the chain lay broken on the ground and the back wheel was completely buckled, looking as if someone had assaulted it with a sledgehammer – or, more likely, with a heavy boot.

Edwin stared at the mangled wreck blankly for a few moments, then turned and walked away.

*

By the time he reached home, Edwin was dripping with sweat. He came in through the front door, dropped his rucksack beside the shoe rack and walked straight out to the kitchen. He filled a pint glass with cold water and downed it in one. It was only then, as he went to refill the glass, that he noticed the evidence of his mother's tussle with a lasagne spattered across the floor and up the wall.

A voice sounded warily from the sitting room. "Who's there?"

Edwin closed his eyes and inhaled deeply. "It's me," he said, barely loudly enough for anyone in close proximity to hear, let alone someone in the next room.

Unsurprisingly, Constance proved once again that her hearing functioned well enough when it suited her. She knew perfectly well that it was her son, but she replied belligerently anyway, "Me *who*?"

Edwin pulled out a large floor cloth from the cupboard beneath the kitchen sink. "Me, Mother," he said wearily. "Just me." He soaked the checkered cloth under the tap.

"Oh, it's *you*!"

Edwin bent down to clear up the lasagne. He managed to scoop up most of the crusted-over pasta with his hands and dropped it into the pedal bin.

"Are you coming in here to speak to me or not, boy?" Constance snapped.

"I'll be there in a moment." Edwin got down on his knees and scrubbed at the floor and wall with the cloth until most of the remnants of the tomato sauce were gone.

"What are you doing out there? Shouting about through the house. It's disgraceful." The fact that she spent most of her life shouting seemed to be a point completely lost on Constance. "Lord knows what the neighbours must think!"

Aside from one particularly stubborn smear on the skirting board – he'd have to attend to that later – Edwin satisfied himself that he'd done the best he could. He stood up, dropped the ruined cloth into the pedal bin and walked out into the hall. He opened his rucksack, retrieved the jigsaw puzzle he'd purchased and slipped it out of the St Joshua's carrier bag. He folded the plastic bag neatly and tucked the precious memento back into the side pocket of the rucksack before trudging through to the sitting room.

Constance was sitting in her armchair surrounded by the remnants of a couple of days' worth of what was patently intended as a display of martyrdom; several empty mugs – one on its side – were on the floor next to her chair, along with a couple of plates and a half-eaten packet of Bourbons that she hadn't returned to the kitchen.

As Edwin walked in with the jigsaw tucked under his arm, she glared up at him. "What were you doing out there?"

"Just clearing up some dropped food."

Constance dismissively waved a hand in the air. "Oh, *that* muck. Well, if you'd left me something sensible to eat then it wouldn't have ended up all over the floor."

Her beady eyes followed Edwin as he walked towards her, set down the puzzle on the floor and started to gather up the plates and mugs.

"Leave those alone," Constance snapped. "I want to talk to you."

Abandoning the crockery, Edwin picked up the jigsaw puzzle and stood up.

"Where have you been?" Constance probed. "And why are you back so soon?"

Even a casual observer would have realised that Edwin resembled a man on the edge. He leaned forward and looked at the puzzle in front of Constance. Almost complete, it showed an image of three Labrador puppies in a basket. "You managed to sort out the bracken then," he said quietly.

Constance frowned. "What on earth *are* you babbling about?"

Edwin nodded towards the jigsaw. "You've got a new one on the go."

Constance scowled at him. "Never mind that. I asked you a question. You said you'd be home on Sunday and today's Saturday. So why are you here?" Her eyes narrowed. "Fall out with your *friend* did you?" she added sarcastically.

"First you don't want me to go," Edwin said wearily, "now you're moaning because I'm back. I can't win, can I?"

Constance's eyes blazed and the vitriol came spewing out. "Don't be so damned insolent! First you leave me here to starve. The fire isn't working properly..."

"The fire? It's the middle of summer, Mother," Edwin interjected.

"How *dare* you interrupt when I'm speaking! You know how I feel the cold with my poor circulation. And thanks to you I've had to sit here freezing to death! *And* I've had to struggle to get upstairs on that wretched stairlift…" Constance trailed off as she saw Edwin looking around the room. "Are you actually listening to a single word I'm saying, boy?"

"Where's your walker?" Edwin enquired calmly.

For a moment Constance looked as if the wind had been taken out of her sails. Then she spluttered, "Oh, yes, that's another thing. One of the wheels on my downstairs walker isn't working properly."

"You don't even use the wheels. You've never used it *properly*. You scrape and clunk it around the house…"

Constance blazed, "Oh, so now you're suggesting I don't know how to use a walker! Well, perhaps if you'd bought me a decent one in the first place it wouldn't be so difficult to use. I told you I needed something sturdier, but oh no, you knew best. As always! And now it doesn't work properly."

Edwin stared at her silently.

"Well?" she said, glaring up at him. "What have you got to say for yourself? Eh, boy?"

"Actually… I couldn't care less."

With sudden ferocity Edwin slammed the puzzle box down on the table, sending the pieces of the jigsaw Constance had been working on flying in all directions.

Constance squealed with alarm. Then, quickly composing herself, she stared at the box. "What's this?"

Edwin turned away and walked to the door. "A present. For you."

Constance glared after him. "Don't you walk away from me! If you think this makes up for what you've put me through the past few days you've got another think coming."

Ignoring her, Edwin crossed to the walker at the foot of the stairs.

Constance peered at the picture on the lid of the box. "Is that Blenheim Palace? You know what an absolutely horrible day out I had there with your father. Why would you choose to remind me of that? You really are the most unfathomably spiteful boy!"

Edwin manoeuvred the walker back and forth a couple of times. There was clearly nothing wrong with it

Constance was almost beside herself with anger now. She screeched at Edwin from the sitting room, "Are you listening to me?"

Edwin pushed the walker to one side. "Don't shout, Mother. What *will* the neighbours think?" He parked the walker against the wall and walked over to collect his rucksack.

"What did you just say to me?" Constance yelled angrily. "Edwin Bartholomew Colthorpe, get yourself back in here this instant!" As if she actually thought it might have some effect, through gritted teeth and with a hint of genuine cruelty, she appended her exclamation with that idle threat only the desperate employ: "Or else!"

Edwin squeezed past the stairlift and without saying another word he wearily climbed the staircase up to the sanctuary of his own room.

CHAPTER 14

Although it had only been the middle of the afternoon, in the haven of his bedroom – a womb of safety away from the vexing tribulations of life – Edwin had drawn the curtains, symbolically putting an end to a truly awful day. Pausing only to pin the St Joshua's carrier bag, the stained handkerchief and the picture of Judy to the wall beside his bed, he'd climbed under the blankets fully clothed, pulled them up over his head and gone to sleep.

There he'd remained for most of Sunday.

Aside from incoherently shouting at him from the sitting room when she'd heard him venturing downstairs at lunchtime to make himself a cheese and pickle sandwich, Constance had been uncharacteristically shrewd enough to leave him alone.

Edwin had spent the entire day immersed in his backlog of unread western novels in a fruitless effort to prevent himself rerunning the events of the last few days over and over in his mind. But even the nail-biting finale of the deliciously pulpy *Kiss Me Once, Shoot Me Twice* failed to engage him; as he reached the last page of the penultimate chapter – in which Deputy Colton Haywood's hunt for diabolical one-eyed bandit Silas Sawyer approached its edge of the seat climax in the maze of caverns near Apache

Creek – Edwin realised he hadn't registered a single word of the last half dozen pages.

By late afternoon he'd had enough of trying to distract his mind and crawled back into bed.

*

Monday morning soon came around and Edwin awoke from a deep, dreamless sleep to the sound of his alarm clock bleeping at him. He couldn't quite believe he'd slept undisturbed for almost 13 hours.

Stepping over his rucksack – which lay beneath the window where he'd dropped it two days ago, its rumpled contents spilling out onto the floor – he opened the curtains for the first time since Saturday afternoon. He was startled to see rain running down the glass. It suddenly felt as if it had been summer forever. How long had it been since it had last rained? He actually couldn't remember.

He peered out at the thick bank of dark clouds. Well, at least it accurately represented his current frame of mind.

Sighing, Edwin made his way to the bathroom, washed and shaved, then returned to his room to dress. He stared at himself blankly in the mirror as he ran a handful of Brylcreem through his hair and combed it into place. The thought of the day ahead filled him with mild trepidation. Then again, it had been a horrible few days and the sooner he got back to his normal routine the better. He straightened his tie. Yes, that was the answer, he decided: bury himself in work. Head down, get on the phone and give that sexist halfwit Dean a good thrashing in sale figures. That would dissipate his melancholia

With slightly more enthusiasm than he'd managed to muster getting out of bed, Edwin bent down, picked up his work satchel and went out onto the landing. No sooner had he got to the top of the stairs than he heard a clunking sound and Constance appeared in the open doorway from her bedroom. Edwin closed his eyes; he really wasn't in the mood for another argument.

Without turning round, Edwin stopped on the first step. "Good morning, Mother."

"So! You finally decide to show your face. I hardly saw sight nor sound of you all day yesterday."

"I was busy."

"Busy? Doing *what*? Wait, don't tell me. Wasting your time on those stupid comic books you read, no doubt."

Edwin sighed and took one more step down the stairs. "They're books, Mother. Western stories. Not comic books." He took another step.

"Wait a moment. Where are you going?" Constance said, frowning at him.

"I'm going to work."

"What about my breakfast?" Constance snapped. "I need to take my pills and I can't until I've eaten. Half an hour *after* food, not before."

Edwin continued down the stairs. "You know where the kitchen is."

Constance's cold blue eyes widened. "I *beg* your pardon?!"

"You managed well enough while I was away, please don't try to tell me otherwise."

"What *has* got into you lately?" Constance's face was turning scarlet with rage. "I've never known such insolence in all of my days, I swear I haven't!"

Edwin had reached the bottom of the stairs. He crossed to the front door. "I'll see you tonight." Pushing his feet into a pair of slip-on shoes, he opened the door. The rain was torrential. He frowned and stepped back inside. As he reached for the large black metal-tipped umbrella propped up behind the door, Constance appeared at the top of the stairs.

"Wait! Edwin…" she called. Was that a rare hint of pleasantness in her voice?

Edwin paused. "Yes, Mother?" he said flatly.

"Please don't you forget to pick up my prescription on your way home."

Please? That was certainly a first.

"I won't."

"And maybe you could pop into Jempson's and pick up some of those delicious jam doughnuts. I know how much you like them. We could have one each for our dessert tonight. That *would* be a treat now, wouldn't it?"

Edwin smiled up at the frail figure at the top of the stairs. Why couldn't she always be like this instead of just turning it on whenever she wanted something? "Yes," he said, nodding. "Yes, it would be a lovely treat, Mother."

"That's settled then," Constance beamed. "Take the money out of my purse. It's on the table in the sitting room."

"That's okay. I'll pay for them. See you later."

He stepped outside, paused on the step to open the umbrella and pulled the door gently shut behind him.

CHAPTER 15

Blake was sat at his desk browsing the Internet, and Ian and Alysson were standing beside the coffee machine chatting when Edwin, dripping wet, arrived at work. Alysson's pink floral brolly was parked in a bucket just inside the door and Edwin dropped his own in alongside it. He pulled out a wet handkerchief from his pocket and dabbed at his face and then, somewhat futilely, the front of his sodden trousers.

Ian looked at him. "Morning, Ed," he said, taking a sip of his coffee.

"Morning," Alysson chimed in cheerfully. "Isn't it horrible out there?"

Mumbling an indecipherable reply – which prompted Ian and Alysson to exchange glances – Edwin walked across to his desk. As he passed Blake, an arm shot out and slapped him hard on the back. "Morning, Eduardo!"

Edwin stared at him blankly.

Blake grinned. His eyes dropped down and he noticed the wet patch on the front of Edwin's trousers. He sniggered. "Oh, bloody hell, sorry mate. I didn't mean to make you piss yourself!"

Edwin continued to stare at Blake, but now his usually dazzling blue eyes were dulled with a trace of silent hatred.

"Oi, Ally cat, look!" Blake said. "Ed's only gone and pissed himself!"

Alysson gave Blake a look of disdain. "Oh just leave him alone." She took her coffee and sat down at her desk.

Blake looked up and noticed the expression on Edwin's face. He bugged out his eyes and with mock innocence said, "What?"

Without saying anything, Edwin turned and crossed to his desk. He glanced up at the sales board. Blake's monthly figure was well above his own.

Blake noticed Edwin looking. "I had a bumper couple of days while you were off, mate," he said with a smug grin on his face. He leant back in his chair. "Looking at your figure, there's not a lot of point you being here really is there?" He looked over at Ian for support.

As Edwin fired up his laptop, Ian stepped over from the coffee machine. "Come on now, Blake. Ed might not be in your league but he gets there in the end." Looking over at the board, he rested a paternal hand on Blake's shoulder. "That said," he continued, "it looks to me like you'll be up for a very nice bonus this month. What you going to spend it on?"

Blake grinned. "Got my eye on some tasty alloy rims for the Beamer."

"Oh, very nice," Ian said. "Keep up the good work and you might even have enough to buy four of them!"

Watching from the other side of the office, Edwin saw Blake's brow crease into a small frown. The idiot doesn't understand, thought Edwin. It actually made him feel a little better.

Ian laughed heartily and slapped Blake on the shoulder. "I'm joking with you, lad." Shaking his head, he walked over to his desk.

"Oh, yeah," Blake said uncertainly. "Er… good one, boss." He swivelled in his chair to face Alysson. "Nice weekend, Ally cat?"

Alysson broke off from typing an email. "Wasn't the weather *beautiful*? Hard to believe it looking out there now." She motioned to the rain lashing against the window. "I went over to Hythe and had a lovely ride in the woods up at Brockhill Country Park."

"Oh yeah?" Blake said salaciously. "I bet you love a good ride, don't you?" He jiggled up and down in his seat.

Alysson rolled her eyes and shook her head.

Blake chortled and shot her a look of innocence that suggested she'd misunderstood. "Hey, so you like straddling big muscular beasts. No shame in that, babe."

"Don't be so childish. You know *perfectly* well what I'm talking about." Alysson returned her attention back to her email.

Blake stretched back in his chair and put his hands behind his head. A self-satisfied expression appeared on his face. "As it happens, I had a good ride myself on Saturday night. Two in fact. Met this blonde hottie down the club in Hastings. My God, she was up for it. So was her cute little friend. A gorgeous redhead. Collars and cuffs matched too." He waggled his tongue at Alysson. "Double-dip Dean strikes again!"

Alysson didn't even look up. "Yeah, whatever," she said with a discernible note of disbelief.

Blake swivelled his chair back round and turned his attention to Edwin. "What about you then, Mr Pissy-pants? You're a bit quiet this morning." Edwin ignored him, but Blake persisted. "Oi, Eduardo! I'm talking to you. Get your dick wet at the weekend, did you?"

Ian looked across from his desk. He tended to tolerate Blake's inappropriate office banter, not only because he was damned good at his job and an asset to the newspaper, but because he quite liked him. He saw a little spark in the younger man which reminded him of the drive he'd had when he was that age. But he had a little red light somewhere in his head that went off when things threatened to get out of hand; there was definitely something not right with Edwin this morning – he was always quiet, but this was something different – and Ian wasn't about to let things escalate to the point they had done last year at the Christmas party. "Okay lads, rein it in. Get on with your work."

Blake – who was all too used to being called out when he took things too far and couldn't care less – smirked to see Edwin visibly bristle at being lumped in with Ian's chastisement.

*

The ethics of snooping around in her son's room had never been open to question as far as Constance Colthorpe was concerned – and she'd have justified her right to do so with her dying breath. After all, he lived in *her* house, didn't he? As far as she was concerned she had every right to know what was going on under her own roof. Aside from the time she'd found that vile magazine hidden underneath his mattress, prying into the minutiae of Edwin's largely insular life had never revealed anything of particular interest, but it gave Constance a feeling of control that she thrived on. But perhaps today that would change. He'd been away for a couple of days and returned in the most deflated mood she'd seen him in for some time. Maybe – just maybe – a little look in his room would furnish her with some juicy tidbit or other, something she could store away and throw back in his face at a propitious moment.

Although her immediate instinct after Edwin left for work had been to go straight into his room and have a nose about, she decided she'd have breakfast first, just in case he unexpectedly returned for something he'd forgotten to take with him; a not infrequent occurrence where the woolgathering wastrel she was ashamed to call her son was concerned.

With a leisurely breakfast of two soft-boiled eggs, a slice of hot buttered granary toast and a mug of tea fortifying her, she made her way up the stairs on the stairlift. When she reached the top, she unbuckled herself from the chair, paused and looked back down the stairs towards the front door, listening intently. Satisfied that she wasn't going to be interrupted, she pushed open Edwin's bedroom door.

Although the curtains were open, the room was quite dark and she switched on the light. Standing in the doorway, the first thing that caught her eye was the sight of Edwin's unmade bed. She tutted. Then her eyes lifted and fell upon the newly arranged Judy shrine. Even though she hadn't been keen on Edwin making pinholes in the walls, she'd allowed him to put up his wretched film posters when he'd asked. But that looked like a plastic bag pinned to the wall. "Surely not!" Squinting, she tottered over to get a better look.

Peering up at the carrier bag – "St Joshua's Hospice Charity Shop," she intoned – her eyes flicked to the soiled handkerchief pinned up next to it. Reaching up, she gingerly felt it, then put her fingers to her nose. She grimaced and recoiled. Turning her attention to the magazine cover, she moved in for a closer look. Pulling a face that relayed her abhorrence she roughly snatched the picture off the wall, tearing it on one edge as she did so. She turned it over and looked on the back, but all it revealed was an advertisement for some charity's monthly lottery.

Then she noticed the stack of paperback novels on the chest of drawers. Dropping the picture of Judy on the floor, she walked over to take a look. She picked through the outrageous titles, with their lurid, violent cover art. "Rubbish," she scoffed. "That boy has more money than sense."

*

As the hands on the clock above the doorway into the *Spectator* office overlapped perfectly to show 12.00, Blake – who'd been watching it for the past five minutes – got to his feet. "Lunchtime!" he exclaimed and walked across to the window. Opening the slats in the Venetian blinds he peered out through the rain towards the sandwich bar on the opposite side of the street. He screwed up his nose. "Bollocks. Still pissing down." As he started to turn away, he glanced down at the courtyard below. "Here, Ed!" he said, barely able to disguise the note of amusement in his voice. "Someone's nicked your bike."

Alysson looked over at him. "Why don't you just give it a rest?"

"No, really," Blake said earnestly. "It ain't down there. Come and have a look if you don't believe me."

Alysson started to get up. "Oh, no, surely not..."

Unable to resist the jibe, Blake said, "Mind you, I can't think why anyone would wanna nick that piece of old junk."

Edwin was staring at his laptop as if in a trance. "I walked in today," he said quietly,

Blake guffawed. "You *walked* here?! In the pissing rain? You must be nuts! No wonder you were wetter than a Nun in a candle shop."

Exhausted by Blake's childish behaviour, Alysson glared at him as if to say 'leave him alone'.

Blake shrugged. "Whatevs."

Pulling a large flask out of her bag, Alysson said cheerfully, "Anyone fancy a cup of tea? Warm ourselves up? It's really chilly in here this morning."

Blake grinned. "Yeah, I thought that to myself earlier, Ally cat looks like she's feeling a bit nippy today." He waggled his eyebrows and nodded his head at the front of Alysson's blouse.

Alysson looked down. Her nipples were protruding through the thin material of her blouse. She tutted. "One of these days, Blake Dean," she said, "you're going to end up in court for sexual harassment."

Blake laughed. "Merely observing the wonders of nature, a perfectly natural bodily response to the cold."

"You were staring at my boobs, you mean."

Blake laughed again. "Not staring. *Observing*."

So, come on, do you want a tea or not?" Alysson said impatiently.

Blake shook his head. "Nah, I think I'm going to toddle over to the road and get myself a ciabbata. I've been starving since I got in. I could really murder a triple meat feast with all the trimmings." He looked over at Ian. "Fancy anything from the sandwich shop, boss?"

Ian took off his spectacles and dropped them on the desk. "Actually, I need to stretch my legs. I think I'll come with you."

Blake cast a quick glance at both Alysson and Edwin. "Can I get either of you ladies anything?"

Alysson shook her head. "No thanks."

Edwin said nothing.

"Suit yourselves." Blake walked over to his desk and pulled his jacket from the back the chair.

Ian came over, slipping on a gabardine overcoat. "When I get back I want to talk to you about the Rye Market. It's coming up to some anniversary or other – I forget which – but I've promised their marketing guy we'd run something next week. Carrie's got her hospital thingamabob, which will take her out of the equation for a bit and I know you've been champing at the bit to express your inner William Shakespeare." He beamed at her. "Thought you might like to take a crack at it."

"Absolutely." Alysson smiled at him appreciatively. "Thank you, I'd love to."

Ian winked at her. "That's hunky-dory then." He turned to Blake and slapped him on the shoulder. "Come on then, wunderkind. That triple meat feast you mentioned has got me salivating. And I've got to nip over to the bank too."

As the door swung shut behind them, Alysson smiled over at Edwin. "Just you and me for tea then, Ed?" She held up the flask.

He looked up at her. "Yes please."

Pulling a mug and a packet of Hobnob biscuits from her desk drawer, Alysson walked over and set down the flask on Ed's desk. "You're ever so quiet today, love. You alright?"

Edwin slid his empty mug across the desk towards her and nodded unconvincingly. "I'm okay."

Alysson unscrewed the lid of the flask and filled Ed's mug to the brim. "I know Blake can be a bit of pain in the backside sometimes, but you really mustn't let him get to you." She poured herself a tea.

Edwin thought for a moment. Then he said, "It's not Blake."

Alysson looked at him sympathetically. "If you want to talk about it? I've got a very good listening ear."

"It's nothing really."

Alysson could sense Edwin wanted to talk, but she didn't want to press. "That's okay. But if you *ever* want to talk about *anything*…"

"I… I met a lady'" Edwin mumbled.

She hadn't expected *that*. "Okay."

"She seemed as though she was really interested at first." Edwin paused.

Allyson pulled Blake's chair over and sat down beside him. "Go on, love."

Edwin faltered. "But then… Oh, I don't know." He sighed.

Putting a comforting hand on Edwin's arm, Alysson said, "You don't have to say anything if you don't want to." Then soothingly, she added, "But if you do, you know I'll keep it completely confidential."

Edwin half smiled at her. She was always so nice to him. "Well," he began, "we spoke on the phone and I arranged to meet her at the weekend."

"And she didn't show up?"

"No, she showed up. We did meet and she was really lovely and we seemed to get along great." Edwin's eyes were moist with tears. "But when I asked her out for dinner her attitude changed completely. She turned me down."

Alysson looked at Edwin hoping that her expression wasn't betraying the mild bemusement she felt. In her not insubstantial experience of dating, what she'd just heard would rank as a file-away-and-move-quickly-on scenario. But she was also intelligent enough to understand that to a man like Ed – at least Ed as she perceived him - it was probably a very big deal. She patted his arm. "I'm really sorry love. It's *her* loss."

Edwin stared down forlornly at his feet and sighed. "Yes, I suppose."

"There's no suppose about it." Alysson smiled warmly. "You're a really nice man, Ed. Any woman would be lucky to find someone like you."

Edwin's mouth creased at the corners and his eyelids flickered. "Thank you."

"Is that a little smile I see?" Alysson took a sip of her tea. "I wouldn't say anything to anyone else, but I've not exactly had much luck in love either. My whole life I've drifted from one bad relationship to another. But you know what? Most of the time I think I'm way better off on my own."

Edwin took a swig of tea. It was hot and sweet and actually made him feel a little better. He reached for the packet of biscuits. "May I?"

Alysson nodded. "Of course."

Edwin took one. "So there's nobody in your life at the moment then?" He crunched on the biscuit.

Alysson shook her head. "Nobody serious. I'm just enjoying being single and having fun."

Edwin sighed. "I wish I could be as philosophical about it as that. But I'm just single and *not* having fun. This woman – her name's Judy – I really thought we had a chance."

Patting his arm, Alysson said, "There are plenty more fish in the sea. I'm sure the right one will come swimming along soon."

"As long as she's not got a tail."

Alysson laughed. She didn't think she'd ever heard Ed joke about anything. "That's a very mermaid-ist remark!"

Edwin smiled at her weakly. "Oops! I suppose it is."

At that moment Blake came through the door holding a sandwich bag and a can of Coke. The shoulders of his jacket looked at if they were probably soaked through to his shirt and his dark hair was hanging in long wet strands across his face. He brushed it away from his eyes. "Bloody hell, it's wetter than a lesbian in a locker room out there."

Alysson and Edwin exchanged a little smile.

Blake went over to his desk and sat down. "You two look pretty cosied up over there. She telling you how bad she wants me, Ed?"

"We'll have another word later, love." Alysson patted Edwin's arm and turned and glared at Blake. "Not everything's about *you*, Blake."

"Oooo, you must have your eye on Eduardo then!" Blake's face filled with delight at the prospect of another opportunity to rib Edwin. "Hang on!" His eyes widened as he waved a finger back and forth between Alysson and Ed. "You two got something going on? Is that it, Ally cat? You and Eduardo been talking sex stuff? D'you want me to go out and come back? How long should I give it? 30 seconds sound about right? Reckon you can last that long Ed?"

Alysson stood up. "You really are disgusting. Why don't you do us all a favour by going out and *not* coming back?"

Grinning broadly, Blake sat back in his chair and opened his can of Coke. He pulled his sandwich out of the bag and took a big bite out it. "Nothing disgusting about sex, Ally cat," he said through a mouthful of chewed up bread and meat. He wiped away a blob of mayonnaise from his lips. "It's bloody great. Unless you ain't doing it right."

"It's all you ever talk about." Alysson gave Edwin a little 'just ignore him' look, picked up her mug and flask and returned to her desk.

Blake took another large bite out of his sandwich. "So what was you and Ed talking about then?" he said, spraying crumbs everywhere. "Looked to me like you were just about to hook up."

Alysson rolled her eyes. "We were having an adult conversation. You know, *adult*? Actually you probably *don't* know.

Blake grinned and waggled his eyebrows. "I was right then. *Adult* stuff." He looked at Edwin. "Was it sex, Ed? C'mon you call tell me, we're all mates here."

Edwin said nothing. He was staring at his computer screen. Had Blake been even slightly observant, he might have noticed Edwin's fists were balled so tight that his knuckles were turning white. But he didn't.

"You enjoy a bit of rumpy pumpy, don't you?" Blake pressed. "That lovely warm feeling as you slip inside? I tell you, them two hotties I had Saturday night couldn't get enough of me. Or each other." He licked his lips. "That little redhead... I tell you, the things she did with her tongue..."

"Dear God!" Alysson exclaimed angrily. "Do you *really* think me or Ed give a flying wotsit about your sleazy little fantasies?"

Taking a swig of Coke, Blake swivelled his chair to face Alysson. "They ain't fantasies, I assure you." An image of his actual Saturday night – spent masturbating furiously over lesbian magazine pictorials – flashed into his mind's eye; he quickly discarded it. "Just saying that my apartment has seen more action than an Amsterdam knocking shop, that's all."

"Yes, well, we don't want to hear about it, thank you very much."

Blake grinned. "Only because you wish it was you." He looked over at Edwin. "You must've had a bird or two back at your place, Eduardo. Unless you live with your mum." He guffawed.

Edwin winced and Blake's eyes widened with delight. "That's it, ain't it? Oh my God! You *do* live with your mum! 'Ere, have you *ever* actually been with a woman?"

Once again, had Blake been savvy he might have noticed that Edwin's face was beginning to discolour. But he was having far too much of a good time. "Can you imagine when you get to the Pearly Gates? St Peter will slap a sticker on your knob – 'Returned Unused'!" Blake cackled. "No, no, wait," he cried, rocking with laughter. "Better than that – 'Mummy's Little Angel'!"

Unlike Blake, Alysson *had* noticed the expression on Edwin's face change. As she opened her mouth to call a stop to Blake's bullying, Edwin suddenly stood bolt upright and slammed his fist down so hard on the desk that his laptop bounced. "I've had just about all I'm going to take of your vulgarity, you *arrogant, juvenile… pathetic* excuse for a man!" He glowered at Blake, his eyes burning with hatred.

Blake looked momentarily taken aback, then burst out laughing. "Fuck me," he spluttered. "Where did *that* come from?"

Edwin grabbed up a stapler from his desk and hurled it at Blake, narrowly missing his head. The smile dropped off Blake's face. "Oi, that could've done some damage, you crazy bastard!"

Alysson could hardly believe what was unfolding in front of her, as Edwin – his fists balled and his hair flapping wildly – strode towards Blake. For a fleeting moment, she thought Ed was going to strike him.

Blake flinched, dropped his can of drink and grabbed up his laptop to shield himself. But Edwin swiped at it with his fist and it flew out of Blake's hands, skidded across the desk and dropped onto the floor with a crash.

Blake tried to get up, but Edwin put a hand on his shoulder and pushed him back into his seat. His eyes filled with fear, Blake stared up at the man towering over him. "For fuck's sake, Ed, it was only a bit of bants!"

Alysson, wide-eyed and dumbstruck, watched as Edwin slowly leaned forwards towards Blake. If she'd been a gambler she'd have bet a thousand pounds there and then that Ed was going to pulverize his nemesis right there in front of her. And, God forgive her, at that very moment she actually *wanted* him to. Her heart rate quickened and deep down in her groin she felt a little thrill of excitement and the sudden urge to urinate.

Edwin put his face right up close to Blake's, so close that their noses were almost touching, and said quietly through gritted teeth, "Bants?"

Blake looked absolutely terrified. "Yeah, mate, bants," he gabbled. "I didn't mean any harm by it for fuck's sake."

Edwin closed his eyes, drew a deep breath and exhaled slowly. Then stood upright and Alysson and Blake watched in silence as he retrieved his stapler from the floor and returned to his desk. He picked up his satchel, crossed to the door, grabbed up his umbrella and casually walked out.

Blake sheepishly composed himself and grinned nervously at Alysson. "What the actual fuck was all *that* about?"

Alysson looked at him with disgust and shook her head. "You arsehole, Blake. You needled him and needled him. It's a shame you didn't get what you deserve."

Blake stared at her as if he couldn't quite believe she wasn't on his side. "Jesus. It's hardly my fault if the guy can't take a joke."

It was still pouring with rain when Edwin stepped outside, almost bowling Ian over in his haste. The older man immediately detected something wasn't right. He stood back to let Edwin pass. "You alright there, Ed?" he said, a genuine note of concern in his voice.

Without meeting his eye, Edwin walked on past. "Ask your protégé," he mumbled.

Ian's slightly perturbed look changed to one of annoyance and he turned away and went inside.

As Edwin was about to cross the courtyard, he paused and turned towards Blake's beloved BMW. Stepping over to it, he flipped up the end of the umbrella and scraped the metal tip along the entire length of the vehicle, leaving a deep gauge in the pristine paintwork.

Back in the office, Blake was standing beside Edwin's desk. He casually pulled a Hobnob biscuit from the packet, broke it in half and popped one piece into his mouth. "I know he ain't exactly Mr

Chuckles round here, but I'd have credited him with a better sense of humour than *that*," he said, smiling thinly. Blake was desperately trying to appear calm and collected, but it was far too late for that; Ed – of all people, *Ed*! – had exposed him in front of Alysson as the cowering weakling she'd probably always taken him for.

Alysson was staring at him shaking her head. She pointed to the laptop on the floor. There was a large crack visible across the screen. "Stop being a dick and sort that out before Ian gets back."

No sooner had the words left her mouth than Ian appeared through the door and stopped short. He looked from Blake to Alysson and back to Blake. Then he spotted Blake's laptop and his face turned to thunder. "What the *hell's* been going on here?"

CHAPTER 16

It took Edwin over an hour to get home. Dripping wet, he threw open the front door and steamed in. Kicking it shut behind him, he threw his satchel and umbrella onto the floor and charged up to his room, taking the stairs two at a time.

He stripped off his wet clothes and dropped them in a pile by the door. He pulled out some fresh clothing from his chest of drawers, but as he started to put them on he noticed the gap on the wall where his picture of Judy had been pinned. Looking on the floor around him, he spotted it laying beside the bed. He bent down and picked it up. His face filled with anger as he saw that it had been torn along one edge. He ran his fingers across the image. Then placing it on the bedside table for a moment, he finished dressing and squatted down to bundle the rumpled clothing back inside his Rucksack. He unpinned the handkerchief from the wall, carefully folded it and tucked it into the inside zip-pocket of the rucksack, slipping the picture in alongside it.

As he turned to leave, Constance – hunched over her walker – appeared in the doorway. How had he not heard her coming?

She scowled at him. "What are you doing home from work in the middle of the day?"

Edwin took a step towards her. "Please get out of my way," he said quietly, but sternly.

Constance's eyes narrowed. "Have you been sacked? Have they finally *fired* you?"

"Mother, I..."

"That'd be just about right for you wouldn't it?" Constance continued contemptuously. "You useless article. And I don't suppose you gave a moment's thought about *me* and picked up my prescription?"

Edwin took another step towards her. "I won't ask you again, Mother. *Move!*"

Resignedly, Constance shook her head. "Where did I go so wrong with you? You really are such a disappointment. I'm ashamed to call you my son, ashamed I tell you. Your father, God rest his soul, would be absolutely disgusted if he could see how you turned out."

Edwin was almost on top of her now. Constance took a couple of paces backwards away from her walker and stopped at the top of the stairs. Edwin stared at her accusingly and her eyes widened as she realised what she'd done. "I told you," she flapped. "It doesn't work properly!"

"Neither of them?" Edwin tried to move around her, but there wasn't quite enough room. As he brushed up against her, Constance took a quick step back. She teetered at the top of the stairs for a moment, then lost her footing. With a horrible shriek she lurched backwards. Her head hit the stairlift with a sickening crack and she plummeted to the bottom of the staircase.

Edwin stared down at her for a moment. Constance's body was horribly contorted, with her left arm – presumably broken – sticking out at an unnatural angle. From where Edwin stood there didn't appear to be any movement and he could see a dark red puddle creeping outwards from beneath her head.

Without the slightest trace of urgency or concern, he slowly descended the stairs, dispassionately stepped over his mother's lifeless body and walked out of the house into the rain.

CHAPTER 17

The ticket office at Rye station was unmanned when Edwin arrived. He looked around for the attendant but there was no sign of anyone and a quick look out onto the platform provided no evidence of any staff presence whatsoever. A glance at the departures board ascertained the next train to Eastbourne was on time and due to arrive at Platform 2 in 7 minutes. He walked back outside to take the footbridge across the track, but as he was about to climb the stairs, he heard a scuffling noise and his eyes darted to the left.

Two youths, one dressed in a hooded sweatshirt and the other in a black baseball cap, were kicking a racing cycle that was chained to the bike rack. Edwin glanced back inside at the illuminated departures board – 'Eastbourne: 6 minutes'. Turning on his heels, he strode over towards the youths. One of them saw him approaching and tapped his mate on the shoulder. "Bruv, someone's coming."

The other youth pulled hard on the cycle's brake cables and yanked them away from the bike as he turned to face Edwin. "Mind your own business, cuz, this ain't got nuffin to do with you."

Edwin, a disgusted look on his face, stopped and examined the scruffy teen. The other boy walked around and stood beside Edwin with his hands in his pockets. "You deaf mate?" he said. "This ain't got nuffin to do with you."

Edwin's lip curled. "You mean 'this *has nothing* to do with you'."

The youth with the brake cables stepped out from the bike rack, slowly wrapping them around his knuckles. "You what?" he snarled.

Edwin looked to his left. The hooded lad was standing three feet away doing his best to look intimidating. He snapped his head back to the first boy. "'This *has nothing* to do with you'," he repeated. "But actually it does. Last week I left my bike here." He pointed to the buckled frame of his old bike, still chained to the rack. "*That* bike. Or what's left of it. And I think I may have just found the culprits."

The boy in the cap laughed. "So?" he snorted.

"*So*, scum like you are a scourge on society and I'm sick to death of it," Edwin growled back.

The boy in the cap lurched forward. "Scum? Who the fuck are you calling scum?!" He raised his hand and whipped the brake cable towards Edwin. He missed and Edwin seized the end of it, rapidly pulling the boy towards him.

With his hand wrapped tight around the collar of the boy's jacket, Edwin pulled his head right up close to his own. Spittle sprayed from his mouth. "You," he snarled. "*You're* scum. Your mate is scum. Chances are your whole family is scum."

The boy tried desperately to pull away as his friend stood there dumbstruck. Edwin tightened his grip and the boy started to choke. With his hair now falling on his face, Edwin continued to rant. "That bike was my father's and your five minutes of fun destroyed a fifty year old family heirloom. And all you can say is 'So'!"

The boy was now gasping for breath and his friend stepped up. "Alright, cuz, you've made your point, let him go," he said shakily.

Edwin turned to face him. "Cuz? What's the matter with you kids today? Doesn't anyone teach you how to speak properly?" He looked over the hooded boy's shoulder through the doors into the concourse. The departure board now read 'Eastbourne: 4 minutes'. With a sudden flick of his arm, he hurled the youth to the ground. The boy's cap tumbled from his head and his partner in crime hastily scrambled to rescue it.

Edwin casually strolled off towards the footbridge and disappeared up the steps as the hooded boy bent down to check on his mate. "Fuck, bruv, that cunt was bear crazy!"

The other youth looked up, watching Edwin cross to the far side platform. Breathlessly he replied. "Yeah!"

*

Although the skies were still thick with grey cloud, the rain had finally blown over on the train journey down to Eastbourne, and at a little after 4 o'clock Edwin emerged from the station and made his way to The Golden Views. He was hoping there'd be a room available, but if not... well, he'd deal with that if it came to it.

His whole demeanour as he turned the corner and the B&B came into sight up ahead was discernibly different compared to his sprightly gait the last time he'd arrived in the town. Had it really only been four days ago? It felt like a lifetime ago. Walking with his shoulders hunched and his head down to the ground, he strolled up to the door and stepped inside.

Just under an hour later, with his room for the night secured, he started on his journey along the Grand Parade towards the St Joshua's Hospice Charity shop. He'd rehearsed the whole impending conversation with Judy in his head, playing out all the variables as to how she might react to what he had to say. The very worst that could happen, he reasoned, was they would part ways amicably and promise to keep in touch. And the best that could happen? It gave Edwin butterflies in his stomach to think about that.

As he approached the shop and saw that there were no lights on, he felt a little nip of concern. Reaching the shop door, he pushed the handle. His face fell. The door was locked. He took a step back and noticed the sign inside the glass that said 'CLOSED'. Another sign just below it displayed the opening hours; alongside Monday it said 9-4:30. He glanced at his watch: 4:57. Damn! What was he going to do now? Stepping forwards, he put a hand up to shield his eyes from reflection and peered through the glass. On the far side of the shop he could see a dim light emanating from the doorway to the back room. Considering his options – which, however he looked at them, probably amounted to having to return early the next morning – he turned and started to walk away.

He stopped a few yards up the road and waited for a car to pass. He was about to step off the kerb when the sound of jangling keys came from behind him. He glanced over his shoulder.

With her back turned to him, a woman – with two bulging carrier bags on the ground either side of her – was locking the shop door. Edwin stared at her and his heart skipped a beat. Was that...? As the woman dropped the bunch of keys into her shoulder bag and bent to pick up her shopping, he saw enough of her face in profile to confirm; it *was* Judy. His timing had been perfect after all.

He started forward and was about to call out to her when he thought better of it. Not here, he thought, not in the middle of the street with people milling about. The things he had to say were private and needed to be said somewhere quiet. Edwin stood and watched as, without even noticing him, Judy walked away up the street. He hung back for a few seconds and then, turning up his collar, he took off after her, making optimum use of the busy crowd to conceal his presence.

*

The bus had been heaving and Judy – along with almost a dozen other passengers, crushed together like sardines – had to stand for the entire run home. By the time she stepped up to her front door she was feeling distinctly frazzled and yearning for a large glass of rum and coke.

It wasn't even quite 6 o'clock, but probably because it had been such a miserable day, the light was already starting to fade. On the opposite side of the road, Edwin peered out from behind a parked white transit van. Getting on the bus behind Judy had been risky, but he'd had little choice. Lady luck had favoured him, however, as it had been standing room only. He'd managed to position himself behind a tall man who'd belligerently decided he was going to read his broadsheet newspaper regardless of the confined space; that selfish attitude had benefited Edwin though, and he'd managed to stay well out of sight. Judy had turned her head in his direction once, but he'd quickly looked down at his feet and when he'd raised his head a few moments later he'd been relieved that she'd not appeared to notice him.

Now he watched Judy intently as she set down her shopping on the front step and started feeling around in her bag for her keys. He looked up and down the road. It seemed to be a very pleasant neighbourhood, with rows of similar-looking properties lining either side, but there wasn't a soul about. Perhaps now was the right moment, Edwin thought. But he'd better be quick; Judy had opened the front door and was gathering up her bags.

As he stepped from behind the van and opened his mouth to call out, the roar of a car engine sounded just off to his right and a shiny black 4x4 came speeding down the road. It pulled up at the kerb in front of Judy's house and two quick blasts of the horn sounded.

Edwin ducked back behind the van as, with one foot inside her front door, Judy stopped and turned round. Cautiously peering out, Edwin saw a man climbing out of the car. Could this be the husband, he thought, and a wave of bitterness and envy for what this man had – what he himself wanted – coursed through him.

"Hold the door! Just coming!" Dave called out to Judy. Edwin watched as the man – not even a particularly good-looking man, in Edwin's estimation – pulled a briefcase from the passenger seat, and there was a little pip-pip sound as he auto-locked the car.

Judy had set down her shopping bags inside the door and Edwin watched with resentment as she walked down the short path to lovingly greet her husband at the gate. He watched them hug, but as they went to kiss, Edwin's eyes filled with despair and had to turn his head away.

*

Judy prepared their evening meal – mushroom surprise, her speciality and one of Dave's favourites – in the company of a generous rum and coke. She set the food down on the table spot on 7.30 and they sat down to eat.

Dave, who'd been buried in paperwork since he'd got home, tucked in with gusto. But Judy merely picked at her food, spending more time tracing the outline of the design around the edge of the plate with her fork than actually eating.

Unseen by either of them, a shadow passed across the window.

"I've got an early start tomorrow," Dave said through a mouthful of food. He swallowed and reached for his glass of water. "I've got to go up to London for a couple of days."

"Oh?" Judy said, unable to disguise the surprise in her voice. Dave always outlined his upcoming week's work schedule to her over Friday night dinner, but this was the first she'd heard about a trip to London.

Dave took a sip of water. "Yeah, Roger managed to get us in on a series of meetings with some American buyers. Paul was supposed to be repping us, but he called in sick this morning – he's been wiped out by that viral thingy. So Roger's asked me to step in."

For reasons she'd have been unable to explain coherently if asked, Judy had been feeling edgy since the incident with that man in the shop on Saturday morning. That look of hurt in his eyes as he'd walked out had stayed with her and even revisited her in her dreams that night. There was no rhyme nor reason to it, but that was how she felt and she certainly didn't relish the idea of not having Dave around at the moment. She forced a smile. "Well that's encouraging, love. It shows he has faith in you. It's about time too."

"Hmmm," Dave said, returning to his food. "I'm not very keen to be honest. I don't have half of Paul's expertise. But I don't want to let Roger down and if I can pull it off it could position JRT up among the big boys. And earn me some brownie points."

Judy put down her fork. "You said a *series* of meetings…"

"Yeah, as I said, it's gonna be an overnighter, I'm afraid. I should be back Wednesday evening though." He suddenly noticed Judy had hardly touched her food. "You not eating?"

"No, I haven't got much of an appetite tonight," she sighed.

Dave frowned. "That's not like you. I hope you're not sickening for something. That virus is doing the rounds."

Judy shook her head. "No, I'm fine. I'm just tired. There's a lot going on at work at the moment. It's been a crazy few days."

Dave reached out and stroked her arm. "Well don't overdo it. You're the lifeblood of that place and you won't be much good to them if you run yourself into the ground."

Judy sat back in her seat and yawned. "I'll be fine. It's my day off tomorrow anyway. I'm going to help Beryl spend some of her birthday money and then we're going for a coffee."

Outside the window, Edwin had been watching silently, the feelings of anger, frustration and, yes, burning jealousy swirling tumultuously in his head. That should be *him* sitting in there at the dinner table. Not that man, who couldn't possibly feel the same way about Judy that he did. All Edwin needed was the chance to make her realise.

Not having noticed the small terracotta flowerpots lined up beneath the window, Edwin moved in a little closer. His foot caught one of the pots and it hit the wall with a dull thud. The rim splintered and it fell over. Edwin stumbled, and grabbed at the wall for support. He froze.

"What was that?" Judy looked across towards the window. It was almost dark outside now.

Dave was just crossing the knife and fork on his empty plate. "What?"

Judy frowned. "That noise."

Dave cocked an ear. "I can't hear anything."

Judy stood up and walked to the window. She put a hand to her brow and squinted out into the evening gloom, her eyes darting back and forth. Unable to see anything, she reached out and swiftly drew the curtains shut.

Crouched low beneath the windowsill, Edwin – who'd been holding his breath for so long that he'd started to feel dizzy and thought he was going to black out – exhaled heavily. That had been way too close for comfort. If Judy had been inside alone, for her to discover him prowling around outside the window would have been bad enough. But with her husband there too, things could have turned nasty.

Steadying his breathing, Edwin stayed hunkered down for almost five minutes before he warily stood up. He quietly uprighted the fallen flowerpot, then walked rapidly across the garden to the gate. Casting a contemptuous sideways glance at Dave's car, he quietly closed the gate and hastened off up the street without looking back.

CHAPTER 18

Dave, wearing only his pyjama bottoms, stood at the sink, vigorously brushing his teeth. There was one at the back that had been twinging sporadically for a couple of days and he made a mental note that he must book an appointment with his dentist when he returned from London.

Judy appeared in the doorway behind him. "Chris is late tonight."

Dave looked at his wife in the mirror. She was wearing the low-cut purple silk nightgown he'd bought her last Christmas. She looked sensational and he felt a little stirring in his loins. He stopped brushing his teeth for a moment. "You need to stop worrying about him," he said through a mouthful of spittle and foam. "He's nearly 18."

"I know," Judy said. "I just get a bit twitchy going to bed not knowing when he'll be home."

Dave spat into the sink. "We can't keep a leash on him. He'll be in when he's in."

As he spoke, the sound of a door slamming echoed up from downstairs. Dave wiped his mouth with the corner of a towel. "He's in."

Chris, with his headphones glued to his ears, locked the front door, slipped out of his jacket and hung it on one of the line of hooks on the wall just inside the front door. As he did so Judy appeared at the top of the stairs. "Lock the door before you come up, love." Unsurprisingly Chris didn't respond. Judy could hear the music seeping through his headphones; it reminded her of the faint thrumming noise of a generator. Moreover, if *she* could hear it that loud, God knows what damage it was doing to her son's hearing. "Chris!" she shouted.

He looked up and saw his mother and pulled one headphone away from his ear. "Hiya."

"Will you make sure you lock up before you go to bed please?"

"Already done it," Chris said. "Just gonna have a snack and watch some telly. *An American Werewolf in London* is just about to start."

Judy remembered Dave taking her to see the celebrated John Landis movie a couple of years back when The Phoenix had hosted a short retrospective of his work. Although Dave had assured her it was a comedy – and to be fair she had laughed several times – some of it had terrified the life out of her. "Well don't stay up too late," she said. "You've got college tomorrow."

"No classes till the afternoon," Chris retorted.

"Just don't stay up too late," Judy repeated, with just enough emphasis that she hoped her son might pay heed.

Chris reluctantly nodded his assent, dropped the headphone back against his ear and sauntered out to the kitchen.

Judy went into the bedroom and closed the door. Dave was already under the duvet and had switched on the small bedside lamp.

Judy kicked off her slippers and climbed into bed beside him. "That boy. He'll have to have those headphones surgically removed if he's not careful," she said disapprovingly. "And the volume! He'll be deaf by the time he's 20."

"Sorry? Pardon?"

"I said he'll be deaf by…" Judy saw Dave grinning at her. "Oh ha-bloody-ha."

Dave chuckled and leant towards her. "Mrs Harrison…" He planted a little kiss on the tip of her nose. "You're turning into an old grump."

Judy punched him playfully on the shoulder. "That's *Mrs* Grump to you."

Dave leant forward again and kissed her on the lips. They broke apart and Judy smiled up at him. "I love you."

"Good." Dave smiled at her warmly. They kissed again, more passionately this time. Dave moved back and looked deep into his wife's eyes. "I love you back." He slipped the strap of Judy's nightgown off her shoulder and ran his fingers lightly downwards across her soft pale skin to the top of her breast, feeling the little goose bumps rise in response to his touch. Without taking his eyes off her, he reached out, felt around for the lamp switch and the light snapped out.

The time on the digital bedside clock read 11:27.

*

After he'd left Judy's house, Edwin had lost track of time for a while. Walking for what felt like hours – in reality it was less than 30 minutes – he eventually found himself at the seafront. He veered off the pavement, stepped onto the shingle and crunched his way down to within a few yards of the water's edge. He looked nonchalantly out to sea. The sky was perfectly clear and he could make out some of the constellations.

The tide was in and the perfect globe of the full moon reflecting on the tranquil water triggered a childhood memory within Edwin; the day Jake Beatty had blacked his eye and he'd been too frightened to go home for fear of the thrashing his father would have given him for getting into a brawl. He'd spent the night huddled up in Iden Wood under the bushes beside Carrick Pond. There had been a full moon that night too and between bouts of fitful sleep he'd watched its magic reflection – bright as a spotlight – on the still water. The next day he'd received double the punishment, not only for getting into a fight but for putting the fear of God into his parents when he'd not come home that night.

Edwin sat himself down on the stones, repositioning his bottom to get himself as comfortable as possible, then drew up his knees and wrapped his arms tightly around them. And there he sat for the next five hours, unmoving, staring out to sea with a blank expression on his face. He was so lost in the moment, he wasn't even aware of the smattering of light rain that blew in just after midnight.

*

The digital clock in Dave and Judy's bedroom changed from 03:00 to 03:01. Having tenderly made love for the first time in several weeks, they'd drifted off in each other's arms and were both sleeping soundlessly.

Outside, the streetlamps clicked off, leaving the moon as the only source of illumination.

Edwin had always liked the dark so much more than the harsh light of day. Darkness comforted him, filled him with a sense of safety and well being that he seldom felt during the daytime. He could move freely about unnoticed in the dark, without too much fear of anyone paying him attention, bothering him, *picking* on him.

Turning up his collar against the cold, he stepped out from behind the transit van parked opposite Judy's house. Looking around to ensure he wasn't being observed, he nipped smartly across the road and dropped to his knees next to the offside front wheel of Dave's car. Pulling his Swiss Army knife from his pocket, he selected the corkscrew prong. Then, once more glancing furtively about, he bent low to the ground and reached under the car. After feeling around for a few seconds, he decided he'd found what he was searching for and made a fast jabbing motion. He quickly stood up, scanned the road one last time to satisfy himself no-one had seen him and took off hurridly down the pavement, disappearing into the night.

CHAPTER 19

As 06:00 appeared on Dave and Judy's digital clock, a soft buzzing sound broke the silence in the bedroom. Dave stirred and opened his eyes. Raising his arm to his face, through bleary eyes he fumbled with his wristwatch and managed to shut off the alarm. He turned his head towards Judy. Fortunately she was still sound asleep. He sat up, leant over and gave her a little peck on the forehead. "See you Wednesday," he whispered and slipped quietly out of the bed.

Half an hour later – washed, shaved and dressed in his best suit – Dave left the house carrying his briefcase. The sun was up, there was a faint chill in the air and as he got into his car he was filled with optimism for the day ahead. He still believed Paul was by far the better man for the job – he had a gift of the gab that Dave envied – but that couldn't be helped now. And he was going to do Roger proud and put JRT on the map.

He dropped the briefcase on the passenger seat and turned the key in the ignition. The engine burst into life, juddered a little and died. Dave tried again, but the same thing happened. Dave's brow furrowed – oh, come on, not today! "Third time lucky," he said under his breath, turned the key and as the engine came to life he gently pressed down on the accelerator a couple of times. Gritting his teeth, he eased his foot off the pedal and this time the engine continued ticking over. Breathing a sigh of relief, he slipped on his seatbelt, cast a quick glance over his shoulder to ensure nothing was coming – at this time of the morning it would be unlikely, but better safe than sorry – he pulled away from the kerb.

The car took off down the road at speed, leaving behind it a small puddle of fluid on the tarmac.

*

Judy woke with a start at around 7.30 to find the bed beside her empty. She reached out and touched the empty space, then rested her head back on the pillow, reflecting on her long and involved dream.

It had been a bad one and even though she was now awake, the remnants clung on, festering, filling her with ill ease. The bit right at the tail end had been worst. She'd been at work and suddenly realised she was on her own. The place was in darkness and stock was strewn everywhere. Judy had tried to put the lights on, but they weren't working. Then she'd seen Beryl looking in at her through the window. She had been shouting something and she was laughing and pointing at something inside the shop. Filled with dread, Judy had tried to leave, but the door was locked. Then she'd heard a noise coming from behind her. She'd turned and stared towards the back room and a silhouetted figure had appeared in the doorway, lit so brightly from behind that she'd had to shield her eyes from the glare. She hadn't needed to see who it was. With every fibre of her being she already knew. But as the figure stepped forward and the face was suddenly illuminated – by what, she didn't know – her insides had turned to jelly. It looked like the actor from the werewolf film, Griffin something or other, the one who'd had half his face ripped to shreds. As he'd advanced towards her, arms extended, eyes pleading, mouth moving in exaggerated slow motion but saying nothing, she'd stood transfixed, realising in that moment that she was going to die.

And then she'd woken up.

Twenty minutes later, she was sat downstairs at the dining table. The morning sun was glaring through the open patio doors and a gentle breeze was wafting in. Still wearing her nightgown and with the disquiet roused by the dream still hovering at the back of her mind, she was idly picking at a bowl of cornflakes and browsing the internet on her mobile phone – looking, but without really absorbing anything.

She was so lost in thought that when the doorbell rang Judy didn't even register the chiming noise at first. It rang again and she looked up at the clock. She frowned and then her expression changed to one of realisation; the Amazon parcel that was supposed to have been delivered the previous day!

She stood up, pulled her dressing gown from the back of the chair and padded barefoot out into the hall, wiggling into the fleecy gown as she went.

She opened the front door and the expectant smile dropped from her face as if she'd been slapped. There on the step, looking slightly dishevelled, was Edwin. He smiled at her warmly. "Hello again," he said softly.

"What...? Why...?" Judy struggled to gather her thoughts. She stared at Edwin in disbelief. "What are you doing here? How did you know where I live?"

Edwin's face maintained its fixed smile. "That doesn't matter right now. What's important is I *am* here and I need to speak with you." He took a pace forward.

Judy stepped back and half closed the door in a defensive gesture. "What's going on? Why are you here?"

Edwin looked her in the eyes. "I can see you're concerned. There's no reason to be." He took another step towards her. "Let me come in and we can talk things through."

Judy's heart was pounding out of her chest and she suddenly felt sick. "Talk things through?" She realised her voice was wavering, but there was nothing she could do about it. "Talk *what* through? There's nothing to talk about." She closed the door a little further, psyching herself up to slam it shut in the man's face if she had to.

"Certainly there is. We need to talk about *us*." Still smiling, Edwin moved forward. "Please. I thought we meant something to each other. I've been waiting all night to see you."

Judy looked at him, utterly bemused. What did he mean, 'meant something to each other'? Composing herself a little, she tried to put a smile on her face, but it simply wouldn't come. "Listen, er... Ted..."

"Ed." Edwin stood looking at her adoringly, his ice blue eyes sparkling with anticipation for what she was going to say next.

"Ed. Yes, of course. Sorry. Look, you're a very nice man. You were very kind to us at the shop, and it was lovely of you to bring me those gifts and invite me out for dinner. But that's it. I'm sorry, I've really not got anything else to say to you."

"But..."

"No." Judy hoped it had sounded as final as she wanted it to. "I think you need to leave now," she said firmly.

Edwin looked at her, his eyes filled with sadness. "Please," he said, a slight tremor in his voice. "Just a few moments. We can sort this out."

Judy started to push the door shut. "Sorry, no. I've got to go now."

Moving so swiftly that if she'd blinked Judy wouldn't have even seen it, Edwin wedged his foot in the jamb of the door. He moved forward. His smile had now faded. Apologetically, but with a discernible hint of menace, he said, "I'm afraid I'm going to have to insist." His arm flew up and he pushed the door so hard that it sent Judy reeling backwards.

Edwin stepped briskly inside and closed the door behind him.

*

Dave could have had breakfast at home. But he'd been hankering a full English for weeks, so he'd factored a stop at his favourite roadside cafe along the A259 into his schedule. An army marches on its stomach; that had been one of his late mother's oft-employed sayings whenever he'd tried to head off to school without having breakfast. They served a satisfying meal like no other he'd ever tasted, and he certainly needed to be fully fed and fit for the day that lay ahead.

Now he was back on the road and making pretty good time. As he took the turn onto the B road that circumvented Blechnum Woods, he accelerated, spurred on by the KISS number blaring out from the stereo. He drummed his hands on the steering wheel and nodded his head in time to the beat of the music, intermittently joining in with verve: "I was made for loving you, baby, you were made for loving me..." He stuck out his tongue, mimicking iconic bass player Gene Simmons.

Suddenly a small deer emerged from the woodland up ahead and scampered out into the road.

Seemingly unconcerned, it stopped and turned to look at the approaching car. Dave locked eyes with it and lurched back in his seat. His arms rigid and his hands gripping the steering wheel like grim death, he slammed on the brakes. Nothing happened. He urgently pumped his foot up and down on the pedal, but it took him only a second to realise it wasn't going to do him any good. He spun the steering wheel and the car veered to the left. The 4x4 skidded off the road, careered sideways down a small embankment and with an almighty cacophony of scraping metal and shattering glass, rolled over onto its roof and lurched to a stop. The wheels continued to spin for a few moments and a jet of steam hissed out from beneath the bonnet.

The deer stood in the middle of the road, curiously observing the upturned vehicle, blissfully unaware of the severity of what had just happened. Then, sniffing briefly at the air, it turned and darted off back into the undergrowth. Everything fell silent, except for the faint sound of music emanating from the stereo. "I can't get enough... no, I can't get enough..."

Dave – upside-down, still seat-belted and with blood dripping from a deep gash on his forehead onto the roof lining – was out for the count.

CHAPTER 20

Judy and Edwin stood facing one another in the hallway. Judy put her hand on the handrail in a defensive stance as Edwin slowly advanced towards her.

He raised his hands to show her he meant no harm. "You don't need to be scared," he said softly. "I just wanted a chance to talk to you."

Judy was indignant. "Scared? You've forced your way into my home... of *course* I'm scared."

Edwin continued to speak soothingly. "You've honestly no need to be." He smiled at Judy and patted at his tousled hair. "And come along now." He smiled, but there was no real humour there. "I didn't exactly *force* my way in."

Judy glanced up the stairs hoping against hope that Chris might appear. No such luck. He could sleep like the dead. Though unable to disguise her fear, she attempted to put on a bold face. "Well what would *you* call it then?"

Edwin, his hands still held out in front of him as if to indicate she has nothing to fear from him, continued to move slowly forward towards Judy. She was matching him step for step, as she backed away through the door into the dining room.

Edwin thought for a moment. "I'd call it..." He paused, searching for the right words. "A golden opportunity. For you and I to get to know each other."

"And coming uninvited into someone's home constitutes a golden opportunity in your head, does it?"

Edwin looked at her with a slightly quizzical expression on his face. Why was she being like this with him?

Continuing to back away from Edwin, Judy cast a quick glance over her shoulder towards her mobile phone, which was sitting on the table beside the half eaten bowl of cornflakes. "I don't understand what you want. Please, will you just leave." As she backed up against the table, she made a sudden grab for her phone.

Edwin lurched forward, snatched it from her and tossed it across the room. It hit the wall and bounced onto the carpet. "No interruptions," he said firmly. "We need to talk. Sit down."

Judy hesitated.

For the first time a crack started to show. "I said sit *down*!" Edwin snapped. He saw the startled look on Judy's face and his ire melted away. "I'm sorry," he said quietly. "Please. Sit down."

Judy couldn't see she had any option but to comply. "Okay listen. If I hear you out, will you go?"

Edwin gave her a little nod and after a moment's pause Judy sat down. As she did so, her dressing gown fell open, revealing her low cut silky nightgown. Even in that moment, where a lot of men might have taken the opportunity to leer, Edwin maintained his gentlemanly values; he averted his eyes. Judy hastily wrapped the gown tightly back around her. "That's a very becoming nightdress," Edwin said, raising his eyes to meet Judy's. "*Très chic*."

"Just say what you've got to say and leave."

Looking about him, Edwin loomed over her. He ran a hand through his hair. "This is very nice. You have a lovely home, Judy."

Confused, Judy stared up at him. "A lovely *home*? What exactly is it you want from me?"

Edwin sighed. "I've not been the luckiest man where... well..." – he raised his hands and made little invisible quotation marks in the air – "...the opposite sex..." – he dropped his hands – "...is concerned." He cleared his throat.

Judy looked at him in silence. Her mind was racing double time.

"I think perhaps it's because I've never met the right woman. I have..." – he paused, once again searching for the right word – "...standards, you see. I've been looking for someone like you all my life."

Hardly able to believe what she was hearing, Judy stared up at him. "You don't even *know* me."

Edwin didn't seem to notice the undisguised note of contempt in her voice. He smiled at her warmly. "We're *meant* to be together, you and I. I just know it, you must feel it too."

Judy shook her head as if she was trying to force herself to wake from a bad dream. "Together? I'm sorry, am I missing something? What are you talking about? Where has all this come from?"

"It was always destined that we would be together," Edwin said, his face brimming with adoration. "The first time I heard your voice I knew you were someone special."

Judy had had enough of this nonsense. The alarm bells of fear were still ringing overtime in her head, but she was starting to feel increasingly angry now. "I'm a married woman!" she exclaimed.

Edwin smiled down at her and gently shook his head. As if it was a response that would change her mind about him, he said softly, "Not any more..."

Judy felt her stomach turn and for the second time in five minutes she thought she might throw up. "What do you mean, not any more?" she cried angrily. "What have you done, you... you *freak*?!"

Startled by her sudden outburst, Edwin took a step back.

Judy was on her feet and glaring at him. "What have you done to my husband?"

Over Edwin's shoulder she saw a movement as Chris, dressed only in his boxers and rubbing the sleep from his eyes, appeared at the dining room doorway. "What's all the shouting about?" he mumbled.

Edwin froze. His eyes widened. It hadn't even occurred to him that there might be someone else in the house. After a fleeting moment of indecision, and without even looking round, he rushed to the open patio doors and out into the back garden.

Unable to withhold a sob of despair, Judy sagged back onto her chair. With a look of genuine concern on his face, in an unusual display of affection, Chris came over and put his arm around his mother's shoulders. "Mum, what's wrong? What's happened? Who was that man?"

Judy managed to compose herself. "Just a customer from the shop. I need to call the police." A look of worried realisation crossed her face. "And I need to call Dad." She got up and hurried over to retrieve her phone.

Chris walked over to the patio doors and looked out. He saw the back gate hanging open. "It's okay," he said. "He's gone."

He turned back to see his mother already had the phone to her ear. "Police?" She paused. "I want to report an intruder."

CHAPTER 21

As had been the case the previous night, Edwin registered little of what had happened to him between taking flight from Judy's house and arriving back at The Golden Views. His mind was in a whirl.

Idiot, Colthorpe. Idiot, idiot, *idiot*! He'd planned his meeting with Judy meticulously, right down to the last cough. He'd thought of everything… except now it seemed he hadn't thought of *everything*. Who had that been in the house with her? The husband? No, it couldn't have been, the car was gone from the front of the house when he'd arrived. His stomach flip-flopped as another possibility occurred to him: Surely not a lover? No, Judy wouldn't do that, it didn't even bear thinking about. Edwin quickly banished the notion from his mind. So… a child then. A boy. Yes, of course, that was it. Judy had a son! It was suddenly so obvious he couldn't comprehend why he'd not realised straight away.

Edwin pushed past the startled landlord, who was on his way out of the front door, and ran up the stairs to his room. He slumped down on the edge of the bed. His mind was spinning, his forehead beaded with sweat and he was struggling to get his breath back. What was his next move to be? The husband should be safely out of the picture, he thought. But what about the son? The idea of abandoning Judy now was unthinkable. There was no doubt in his mind that, if they hadn't been disturbed, if he had been able to spend just a few more minutes speaking with her, she'd have realised the obvious: They were destined to be together. He stared at the floor, desperately trying to decide what to do next. And then an idea popped into his head.

*

Her phone pressed to her ear, Judy was sitting at the dining room table with Chris. She shook her head and tapped the 'end call' option. "It just keeps going to answerphone."

Although Judy hadn't explained to him what was going on, Chris realised it had to be bad. He'd only ever seen his mother cry once before in his entire life and that had been when Granddad passed away. "Try his office," he said.

"He's not in the office today. He's gone to London for a meeting."

Chris's face registered a trace of relief. "Well that's it then!" he exclaimed. "He wouldn't answer if he's driving."

Judy looks at the clock. "He should be there by now though," she said, struggling to hold back the tears. "I'm really worried. Something's happened to him."

"You're not making sense, Mum. What's going on? *What's* happened to Dad?!"

"I don't know." Judy buried her head in her hands. "But *something* has, I just know it."

As Chris reached out to comfort her, the doorbell rang. Judy looked up. "That'll probably be the police."

Chris stood up. "I'll get it."

*

With his rucksack slung across his shoulder, Edwin emerged from his room. Hearing muffled voices and the sound of feet on the stairs, he stopped at the banister and peeped over the edge. His eyes widened. There were two uniformed police officers – a man and a woman – coming up the staircase. Quickly, but as quietly as possible, Edwin crossed the landing back to his room, but as he stepped inside and turned to close the door the two officers reached the top of the stairs.

"Excuse me. Mr Colthorpe?" the male officer called out.

After a moment of hesitation Edwin opened the door wide and smiled at them nervously. "Yes, that's me."

The two officers crossed the landing towards him. The female said, "I'm Constable Carter, this is Constable Banks. May we have a quick word with you please?"

"About what?" Had that come out a little too defensive?

The woman gave him a half smile. "We'd rather not discuss it here, sir."

Edwin frowned. Be calm, you've done nothing wrong. "What's going on?" he asked, as nonchalantly as possible. "What's this about?"

Banks spoke again. "Would you mind accompanying us to the station, sir?"

Edwin's mind was racing. "I'm actually quite busy, can't you just tell me what you want?"

The two officers exchanged glances. "We'd be much obliged if you could just come along with us," Carter said. She smiled at Edwin. "I assure you we'll not take up too much of your time."

Realising he had little choice but to comply, Edwin nodded his consent. "Very well," he said with an evident note of impatience in his voice.

Banks smiled appreciatively. "Thank you, sir. As my colleague said, we won't keep you long."

Edwin pulled the door shut behind him and followed them down the stairs. Standing at the bottom of the staircase, the landlord watched them descend and as they passed him by he smiled and nodded obsequiously at the two officers. His gaze followed them as they helped Edwin into the car. He'd seemed like such a nice man too, the landlord mused.

*

At the same moment that Edwin stepped out of the front door of The Golden Views, Judy was pointing to the computer screen in the back room at the shop. "That's him," she said. "The man with the flowers."

The female police officer sat forward and squinted at the screen. "CCTV can be so indistinct," she said. "You should see some of the images we're expected to work with." She smiled. "But they've improved in leaps and bounds over the past couple of years. Yours is really good."

"It was only installed last year."

"Okay. So this was…" – the woman glanced at her notepad – "Saturday?"

Judy nodded.

"Can you tell me again what this man…" – she glanced at her notepad again – "…Ed wanted?"

"He gave me the flowers and asked me out for dinner."

"And when you refused?"

Judy rubbed the side of her face. "He looked disappointed, but he left."

"And he didn't threaten you or say anything to make you believe you might be in danger?"

"Not then, no. As I say, he just left. But this morning when he turned up at the house his whole manner was threatening." Judy could feel the tears welling up in her eyes. "He forced his way in and he was talking rubbish, something about us being destined to be together. And he also implied that he'd done something to my husband. If my son hadn't been home I'm not sure what would have happened." She looked at her watch. "God, my friend is coming round to meet me in half an hour, we're supposed to be going out. Not that I'll be going anywhere today now."

The officer smiled at Judy and rested a hand on her arm. "Don't worry. We're all done here for now. I'll take you home."

Judy returned the smile. "Thank you, Officer…?"

"Gallagher. *Constable* Gallagher."

"Thank you, Constable Gallagher. You've been very kind."

*

The short journey in the car to the police station had passed in silence and given Edwin time to think. Whatever Judy may have said to them – and he was confident he'd done nothing that might constitute a crime – could be explained. The only thing he couldn't understand was why they hadn't just asked him their questions back at The Golden Views.

When they arrived at the police station, the two officers took Edwin past a reception desk – the sergeant on duty didn't even look up – and along a short corridor to a room at the end.

The walls were painted a pleasing shade of green; green had always been one of Edwin's favourite colours. Other than a table with two chairs positioned on either side, the small room was bare.

Constable Carter closed the door behind them and Constable Banks invited Edwin to take a seat. Edwin nodded a thank you and sat down, while Banks settled himself on the opposite side of the table.

"Can I get you a cup of tea?" Carter asked. Edwin shook his head. "No thank you."

Carter moved round the desk and sat down next to her colleague. Edwin looked at them enquiringly. "Can you please now tell me what this is all about?"

Carter spoke. "Could you please confirm that your address is number 4 Hornbill Close, Rye?"

Edwin was beginning to feel a little impatient. He really didn't have time for this. He had things to attend to. "That's correct."

"And you live there with your mother, Mrs Constance Colthorpe?"

"I do."

Banks took over. "Unfortunately at 8 o'clock this morning your neighbour, a Mrs Baker, dropped round to see your mother and found her laying at the bottom of the stairs. Mrs Baker immediately called for an ambulance, but I'm very sorry to have to inform you that your mother was pronounced dead at the scene."

Edwin simply stared at them without a trace of emotion on his face. The two officers exchanged glances; did he understand what they'd just told him?

"What am I supposed to do now?" Edwin muttered dispassionately.

Carter cleared her throat. "Your mother's body has been taken to Conquest Hospital in Hastings. We would suggest you make your way back to Rye and contact the local authorities." She slid a sheet of paper across the desk. "All the information you need is on here."

Barely affording it a glance, Edwin picked it up, folded it in three and tucked into his inside jacket pocket. "Is that all? Can I go now?"

Unable to disguise his puzzlement at Edwin's complete lack of emotion, Banks rose. "Certainly, sir."

Edwin stood up and Banks motioned him to the door. "We're so sorry for your loss, sir."

"Thank you." Edwin forced a brief smile. "Do you have somewhere I could wash my hands?"

"Of course." He pointed down the corridor. "Second door on the right." As Banks stood and watched Edwin disappear into the toilet, Carter stepped up alongside him. "Bugger me, Sandra," Banks said with a sigh. "I've been on the force for 11 years and I've had to hand out more than my fair share of bad news. I thought I'd seen every reaction on the spectrum. But *that*..." – he motioned towards the toilets – "...well, that was a first. I wasn't even sure he took on board what I'd said. I mean, you tell someone their mother just died you expect *something*. He just stared at us."

The toilet door opened and Edwin reappeared. He raised a hand of acknowledgement to the two officers. Carter nodded at him and Banks put up a hand and followed Edwin down the corridor towards the exit.

As Edwin reached the reception desk, Constable Gallagher – the female officer who'd reviewed the St Joshua's CCTV footage with Judy – appeared through the main entrance. Edwin passed her and she did a little double-take.

Banks stepped up to her. "Alright there, Alex? What news from the charity shop?"

"Who's that man?" Gallagher said, turning to see Edwin disappearing through the door.

"Mr Colthorpe? A neighbour found his mother dead early this morning. A bit of an oddball if you ask me. He didn't react like anything *I've* ever seen before. In fact, he didn't seem that interested at all."

In the time it took Banks to reply, Gallagher had spun round and was heading for the door after Edwin.

Banks frowned. "Why, what's going on?"

"He looks just like the guy from that incident at the charity shop," Gallagher shouted back over her shoulder. "Colthorpe you said?"

"Yeah. Edwin Colthorpe."

Gallagher ran out onto the steps. There was no sign of Edwin. The door swung open behind her and Banks appeared. "He's gone," Gallagher said breathlessly.

Banks pointed. "There!"

Gallagher followed his gaze and caught a glimpse of Edwin as he appeared from behind a parked lorry and stopped at the kerb waiting to cross.

"Mr Colthorpe!" Banks started forward.

Edwin glanced back over his shoulder. He saw the policeman coming towards him, turned away and started to walk off up the pavement.

"Mr Colthorpe!"

Edwin quickened his pace. Banks, with Gallagher hot on his heels, scooted up the pavement after him. "Mr Colthorpe," Banks shouted again. Edwin suddenly stopped still in his tracks. He didn't turn round. Banks ran up and came to a halt alongside him. "Sorry sir, would you mind coming back in for moment please? I've just got a couple more questions I wanted to ask you."

Edwin shot a look at Gallagher as she approached. "Is this really necessary. I'm a very busy man." He tried to maintain his nonchalant demeanour, but it was more than evident that he was now looking slightly rattled.

"Please, sir," Gallagher said. "We won't keep you long."

CHAPTER 22

Judy had got home just in time to find Beryl on the doorstep. She'd made her apologies and told a concerned-looking Beryl that she'd explain why she'd just rolled up in a police car once they got inside.

Now she was sitting at her kitchen table with her head in her hands, while Beryl stood at the worktop filling two mugs with steaming coffee. She looked at Judy with concern. "You going to tell me what's going on then, love? I thought we were going *out* for coffee?"

Judy looked up at her friend. "I'm really sorry. It's been a horrible morning. I had to go into the shop and review some CCTV footage with a policewoman."

Beryl's face dropped. "Oh no! Someone didn't break in did they?" She set down a mug of coffee in front of Judy.

"No, nothing like that. It was..." Judy paused. She took a breath. "You know that guy who came into the shop and made the donation?"

Beryl chuckled. "What, the jigsaw puzzle guy? Your fancy man?"

"It's not a joke, Beryl!" Judy said angrily.

The smile melted from Beryl's face. She'd never seen her boss – her *friend* – like this before. "Sorry."

Judy saw the expression on Beryl's face. "No, *I'm* sorry," she said. "I didn't mean to snap. But that man, he came to the house this morning and forced his way in. He seems to have it in his head that we're... well, romantically linked."

"*What*?!" Beryl exclaimed. She set down her mug and took a seat.

Judy sighed. "I didn't say anything at the time, I was a bit shocked to be honest. But you know when I had those flowers and chocolates in the shop on Saturday morning?"

"Of course."

"Well they were from *him*. He came in and asked me out to dinner."

"What did you say?"

"Well, I told him I was married, obviously. But somehow he found out where I live and turned up on the doorstep. He was spouting all sorts of nonsense about destiny and me being his perfect woman. He's some sort of unhinged stalker. It was terrifying. If Chris hadn't been here, God knows what would have happened."

Beryl looked stunned. She'd enjoyed the little wind up, but what she was hearing now... well, it defied credence. "That's unbelievable! Where's Dave?"

Judy felt herself starting to tear up again. "That's the thing. I don't know. He's supposed to be in London, but I haven't been able to get hold of him. I'm sure that man has done something bad. Honestly, you hear stories about people like him and you just think they must be exaggerated." She quickly brushed a tear off her cheek. "And now it's happened to me."

*

Edwin was seated alone in the interview room at the police station; its walls were no longer a pleasant shade of green after all, he mused. He'd been waiting there for almost fifteen minutes and very noticeably there'd been no offer of refreshment this time.

The door opened and Gallagher and Banks came in. Without saying a word they walked over and sat down opposite Edwin. Gallagher placed a cardboard folder on the table in front of her.

"Should I be calling a lawyer?" Edwin said amicably, without revealing so much as a hint of the impatience that was beginning to fester.

"Do you think you might need one, sir?" Banks replied.

Edwin frowned. "I don't know. *Do* I?" The two officers looked at him. There was a pregnant pause, then Edwin beamed. "I was joking. It's just that I've got important things to do. And as you're well aware I have to get back home to see about my mother."

"If you could just bear with us, Mr Colthorpe, this hopefully won't take long." Gallagher pulled out her notebook from the folder. "Do you know a Mrs Judy Harrison?"

Edwin didn't hesitate. "Yes I do." He smiled confidently.

"How *well* do you know her?"

Edwin sat back in his chair. He looked Gallagher in the eyes. "We've just recently started seeing each other."

"I see." Much as she didn't want to, Gallagher had to avert her eyes from Edwin's piercing stare. She looked down at her notebook. "I have to tell you, sir, that there has been an allegation made against you that suggests otherwise."

Edwin sat up straight, an expression of surprise on his face. "Allegation? By whom? I don't understand. What sort of allegation?"

Gallagher cleared her throat and glanced at Banks. He gave her a little nod and she turned back to look at Edwin. "Mrs Harrison has reported that at a little after 8.00 am this morning, you forced your way into her house, you behaved inappropriately towards her and that you implied you have harmed her husband, Mr David Harrison."

"Behaved *inappropriately*?" Edwin eased back in his chair again, an expression of mild amusement on his face. "Well, obviously there must

be some sort of mistake. Judy – that is, Mrs Harrison
– and I are very much in love."

Banks sat in silence, observing Edwin. In
light of Mrs Harrison's statement, he thought the man
was displaying an unnatural calm.

Gallagher leant forward, a look of doubt on
her face. "In love, sir?"

Edwin nodded. "Oh yes. Very much so."

"I put it to you, sir, that you've adopted
some kind of unhealthy obsession with Mrs Harrison
and it's very much a one-sided situation. You have
violated…"

Edwin shook his head. "No," he muttered.

Gallagher ignored him. "…*and* intimidated
her, both in her own home and at her place of work."

Edwin shook his head more vigorously.
"No. No, no, no."

Gallagher sat back. "No… *what*, Mr
Colthorpe?"

"No to all the things you just said.
Intimidation. Violation. I did none of those things."

"So you're saying you didn't visit her at the
St Joshua's Hospice Charity shop?" She produced a
photograph from the cardboard folder and slid it
across the table towards Edwin. "Or force your way
into her home?"

"Force my way…? No, of course I didn't."
Edwin glanced at the photograph. It showed a slightly
grainy image of himself at the counter in the shop,
presenting Judy with the bunch of flowers.

He pushed the photo away. "We've met up on several occasions. She was always pleased to see me, not intimidated."

Gallagher slipped the photograph back into the folder and tapped the cover of her notebook. "In the formal complaint Mrs Harrison has made about you, she stated she has done nothing to encourage the unwanted attention you have given her."

The corner of Edwin's mouth twitched. "Well, of course she'd say that." He leant forward conspiratorially and in hushed tones, as if he were breaking a confidence, he whispered, "She doesn't want her husband to know about us."

Gallagher and Banks exchanged glances. Edwin could detect the air of disbelief. He raised a finger to his lips. "Ssshhhh."

Gallagher looked at him quizzically. "Are you suggesting that yourself and Mrs Harrison are actually involved in a consensual relationship?"

Edwin sat back in his seat again. He was beginning to look very pleased with himself. "I'm not *suggesting* anything. I'm telling it as it is." He smiled. "You don't think I'd come all the way down to Eastbourne in pursuit of a woman who wasn't interested, do you?"

"What makes you think Mrs Harrison was 'interested'?"

"Well, she er..." Edwin looked thoughtful, "she telephoned me. And when we met in the pub there was no doubt whatsoever about her feelings."

Gallagher frowned. This wasn't going the way she'd expected it to. "Do you have any evidence of this call, sir?"

"Absolutely." Edwin reached into his pocket and withdrew his mobile phone. "It'll be in my call history. It was exactly one week ago." He scrolled through the list of recent calls and stopped at the previous Tuesday afternoon. "There it is."

Gallagher held out her hand. "May I?"

"Certainly." Edwin handed his phone to her.

She took a look at the screen and then jotted down the details of the number, the date and the length of the call in her notepad. She passed the phone back to Edwin. "Thank you."

Edwin smiled and tucked it back in his jacket pocket. "Is that everything then?" he said, as if there was no doubt in his mind that the conversation was over.

"Can you just wait here for one moment please, Mr Colthorpe," Gallagher said.

Edwin sighed. "Very well. But…"

"We'll only be a minute." Gallagher and Banks got up and left the room, pulling the door shut behind them.

In the corridor outside, Gallagher let out a long, slow breath through gritted teeth. "What do you think?"

Banks frowned. "I don't like him. I don't like him at all. But that doesn't make him a crim." He sighed. "He seems pretty damned sure of himself."

"Agreed," Gallagher said. "But something's clearly not quite right."

"No doubt about that." Banks looked puzzled. "But you do have to wonder why Mrs Harrison failed to mention that she'd phoned him."

"I know. I'll speak with her again. But what do we do with him now?"

Banks shrugged. "No reason to hold him. We have let him go."

CHAPTER 23

Any suggestion that he'd behaved inappropriately having now been quelled, Edwin walked out of the police station lighter of heart than he'd felt for several days. Yes, that sceptical police officer – he hadn't liked her at all – had told him it would be in his best interest to stay away from Judy from now on. And yes, he'd said he would comply... sort of. What he'd actually done was assure her once again that there had been a misunderstanding and that he would not be making any unwelcome advances. *But...* what if Judy *agreed* to meet him? That would be different, wouldn't it? Then nobody could accuse him of non-compliance over what, at the end of the day, was only a recommendation, not an enforcable order.

The policewoman had offered to drive Edwin back to his B&B, but he'd politely declined. It was a beautiful day, he'd told her, and he was an avid wayfarer.

Making his way down Lottbridge Drove in the direction of the seafront, he passed an eatery and stopped to look at the meal deal poster in the window. He'd never had much interest in takeaway food, but suddenly he found himself salivating over the idea of some southern fried chicken and a large portion of chips.

He emerged a few minutes later clutching a large paper bag. Cutting across to Princes Park, he found a nice spot on the grass beside the boating lake and sat in the warm sunshine to eat his lunch and formulate his next move.

Twenty minutes later he'd come to a decison. Wiping the grease from his fingers and tucking the used paper napkin into the bag with the uneaten remains of his meal, he located a wastebin. Then, sitting back down on the grass, he pulled out his mobile and called the number for St Joshua's.

Sylvia was alone in the shop when the phone rang. Having just got down on her knees to unpack some boxes of donations, she tutted. "You couldn't have called two minutes ago, could you?" she mumbled, grimacing at the spasm that ran through her leg as she got up. "Oh no, that would have been far too much to ask for." She stepped over to the counter, picked up the receiver and said chirpily, "Good afternoon, St Joshua's Hospice, Eastbourne."

Edwin sat himself up. "Good afternoon. May I speak to Judy Harrison please?"

"I'm sorry, she's not working today. Can I help at all?"

Edwin's mind raced. Come on, man, *think*. "Oh, er, yes, I hope so." He looked quickly about the park and his eyes fell upon a small shack selling ice creams and confectionary; the colourful sign above the open counter front said 'Downes & Son'. "My name is Officer Downes. I'm calling from Eastbourne police station. We need to speak to Mrs Harrison on a matter of some urgency. Would you have her home number to hand please?"

"Oh, yes, certainly. One moment." Although she'd had no idea what was going on – Judy had said she would explain later – Sylvia had been worrying about her manager since she'd dropped into the shop with a police officer that morning. She opened a drawer beneath the till and pulled out a dog-eared post-it note. "I've only got her home number I'm afraid. It's…"

Edwin listened, committing the number to memory. "Thank you very much, you've been most helpful. Goodbye." Edwin smiled with satisfaction and stretched back on the grass.

*

Judy had tried everything she could think of to reach Dave. Chris had offered to stay with her, but she'd insisted he go to college and promised to contact him as soon as she knew anything. Besides, Beryl was there so she wasn't alone. She'd managed to get hold of Dave's boss Roger at JRT, who'd said he would contact the hotel where the business meeting was set to take place. "Don't worry," he'd told her, "I expect he's just forgotten to switch his mobile on." Judy had agreed, although she knew that Dave would never do that; his mobile phone was like an extension of his right hand. Roger had promised to call her back.

She was sitting on the sofa with Beryl when the landline phone rang. She jumped up and she grabbed up the receiver. "Roger?"

Edwin, laid on his back staring at the clouds, said quietly, "Don't hang up."

Judy's expression froze. She mouthed silently at Beryl, "It's *him*!"

Beryl frowned and was about to ask who she meant when the penny dropped. Her face darkened and she sat forward on the sofa.

"What do you want?" Judy said as calmly as possible, though there was clearly a discernible tremor in her voice.

"I'm sorry about earlier," Edwin said. "I didn't mean to scare you, I just wanted to talk."

Judy said firmly, "I reported you to the police."

"I know." Edwin paused. "Don't worry, I've spoken with them and I forgive you. It was just a misunderstanding."

Judy picked up the base unit of the phone and carried it to the sofa. She sat back down and held the receiver so that Beryl could lean in and listen. "How did you get my number?"

"Don't worry about that now."

"Of course I'm worried!" Judy exclaimed. "Why are you ringing me, why can't you just leave me alone?"

Edwin sighed. "I keep trying to tell you, I just want to talk."

"There's only one thing we have to talk about." Judy was getting angry now. "What have you done with my husband?"

"If you'll just meet me, I'll tell you everything."

Beryl's eyes widened and she shook her head silently mouthing 'No'.

Judy's brow furrowed. "Why on earth would I meet you?"

Edwin spoke softly. "Please, I just need to explain. About your husband. About *everything*. If you meet me and just listen to what I have to say you'll..." – the words stuck in his throat – "You'll never see or hear from me again."

Judy paused, her brain ticking over. Then she nodded. "Where and when? It has to be somewhere public."

Beryl looked at her friend as if she'd gone completely mad.

Edwin beamed and sat up. "Do you know the little café on the cliff?"

"The one at Beachy Head?"

"Yes. Meet me there at 5 o'clock. Just you. No-one else. And no police."

"Okay. 5 o'clock."

Edwin's heart was pounding so fast that he thought it actually might burst. "Thank you, Judy. I promise you won't regret it." He tapped his phone to end the call.

Judy put down the receiver and returned the phone to the table. Beryl was staring at her in disbelief. "What on earth do you think you're doing? You *can't* meet him, you just can't!"

Judy stood up. "I have to find out what's happened to Dave. And he's promised he'll leave me alone if I do."

Beryl scoffed. "Surely you don't really believe that do you?"

"No." Judy shook her head. "I don't. But what choice have I got?"

Beryl got up, marched over to the table, lifted the telephone receiver cradle and held it towards Judy. "You call the police."

Judy took the receiver from her and returned it to the cradle. "I'm going to meet him. Once I know what he's done to Dave, *then* I'll call the police."

There was a moment's silence, then Beryl said, "Okay. But I'm coming with you. I'll drive you up there."

CHAPTER 24

As he had walked more or less the same route up to the cliffs a few days earlier, Edwin covered the distance from Princes Park to Beachy Head in good time. But by the time he arrived the weather had taken a turn for the worse; the wind was gusting, the blue skies were gone – now masked by a blanket of foreboding grey –and there was the first trace of light drizzle in the air.

There wasn't a soul around and much to Edwin's consternation the cafeteria was closed. With his collar turned up against the cold, he took shelter beneath the awning that was being relentlessly battered by the wind. He went to the door and pressed his nose up against the glass. No activity. Then he spotted the opening times on the door and the words 'Tuesday: Closed'.

Catching sight of his reflection, he realised how windswept his hair looked. He ran a hand through it and patted it into place in an attempt to tidy himself up a bit, but when he stepped out from underneath the awning it simply blew back into its unkempt state. He walked around the side of the café to check the car park at the bottom of he slope. From where Edwin stood it looked deserted; no, wait, not *quite* deserted.

There was a small blue Fiat Panda just pulling in. Edwin glanced at his watch: Two minutes to five.

Fine rain cascaded down the windscreen as Beryl pulled into a parking space and switched off the engine. She gave the wipers a quick swish on double speed and then flicked them off. She turned in her seat to face Judy. "I still think it's a mistake not to call the police."

"He said no police."

"Never mind what *he* said," Beryl exclaimed. "He's clearly not right in the head."

Judy sighed. "I know. But I can't jeopardise the one chance I have to find out what's happened to Dave. I just can't."

Beryl was adamant. She looked up towards the café. "I get that. But I still think this is a bad idea. At least let me walk up with you. I can hang back."

Judy shook her head. "He said alone." She saw the look on her friend's face. "I'll be okay," she said, putting a hand on Beryl's arm. "Honestly, I can handle this. You get yourself off home."

Beryl's face dropped. "I'm *not* leaving you here on your own! I'll wait here."

"Really, it's fine." Judy forced a smile. "*I'll* be fine."

"Ok, well I'm not going home. Call me when you've spoken to him and I'll come back for you."

Judy assented. "Okay. Thank you." She unclipped her seatbelt, opened the door and climbed out of the car. A gust of wind caught her hair and she brushed it away from her face. Then she leaned back into the car. "I've no idea how long this is gong to take though."

"It doesn't matter," Beryl said firmly. "Just call me straight away."

Judy raised a hand to her friend as she pulled away. Taking a deep breath, she turned and began to walk up the slope towards the cafeteria, where she could now see the figure of a man waiting.

As soon as she cleared the car park, Beryl executed a three-point turn and returned. She switched off the engine and peered through the rain, her face filled with concern as she watched Judy making her way towards the café.

Judy could see Edwin beckoning to her to hurry and she didn't need much prompting. With the wind and rain whipping her hair, she picked up her pace, striding purposefully up the slope towards him and the shelter of the café.

Edwin watched Judy approach and he stepped back under the awning, quickly trying to pat his hair back into place. By the time Judy reached the café, she was already sodden. She stopped a few yards away from him and pushed her wet hair back out of her face. "Right, I'm here," she said curtly. "So come on, say whatever it is you've got to say."

It was as if Judy hadn't even spoken. Edwin beamed at her, his face filled with adoration. "Thank you so much for coming," he said jubilantly. "But what an absolutely foul day it's turned in to. And it was so nice earlier. I actually sat in the park and…"

Judy cut him off. "I didn't come here to chit-chat about the weather."

Again, it was as if Edwin was on a preset course from which he wasn't going to deviate. But he did take pause. He cleared his throat. "Yes, well, I just wanted to apologise for my appearance." He ran a hand through his hair. "The rain caught me out. I'm afraid I look a bit of a mess." He smiled at her. "You look beautiful though. Your damp hair is very…" He tipped his head to one side and looked at her thoughtfully, searching for the right word. He made up his mind. "Becoming. Yes. *Very* becoming." He took a pace towards her.

"That's close enough!" Judy exclaimed, stepping away from him.

Edwin stopped. "There's no need to be frightened. I keep trying to tell you, I'm not going to harm you." He smiled. "I was intending to buy you an ice cream, but…" – he pulled a 'typical, isn't it?' expression and gestured to the sign on the cafeteria door – "…as you can see it's closed."

Judy wasn't prepared to listen to any more small talk. "Where's my husband?" she demanded.

Edwin's smile lingered on his lips for a few seconds and then faded. "Don't be angry."

"Don't be...?!" Judy's face was filled with incredulity. "Just tell me where he is!"

Edwin's face darkened. "I don't know."

She hadn't expected that. Judy scowled at him. "Oh no, you're not getting away with that. You got me up here, you know *exactly* where he is and you're going to tell me."

Edwin looked at her innocently and placed a hand to his chest. "Hand on heart. I have absolutely no idea where he is."

"You implied you'd done something to him," Judy snarled through gritted teeth, struggling to keep a leash on her temper. "Now *where* is he?"

Edwin's face suddenly brightened. "Let's walk."

"Let's *not*. Just tell me."

Ignoring her, Edwin stepped out from beneath the awning and began to walk away. He inhaled theatrically. "The sea air is bracing, isn't it? Exhilarating!" He looked back over his shoulder and motioned to her to follow. "Come on," he said jovially. "Stop lollygagging." With that he turned his back on her. He said the word again, accentuating every syllable: "Loll-ee-gagg-ing. Funny word, isn't it?" He chuckled. "My Mother used to say that to me all the time."

Judy was beginning to realise that agreeing to meet this man had been a mistake. If he knew where Dave was – and intentionally or otherwise he'd planted a seed of doubt in her mind as to whether he actually did – he probably wasn't going to tell her. But she had to be absolutely certain. She looked desperately around her. Several hundred yards away near the cliff she could see an elderly man struggling with his dog's harness, but otherwise there wasn't a soul about. She watched Edwin walking up the slope away from her and made a decision. "Wait!" She scurried out from under the awning and caught up with him.

She was walking parallel to Edwin, several yards to his left, but although he was aware of her in his peripheral vision he didn't look at her. He inhaled again, even more theatrically. "It's beautiful up here, isn't it? Even in the rain. I came here once as a child, you know. My Grandmother brought me here for a picnic." A fleeting faraway look appeared in his eyes. "I loved my Grandmother."

The wind was taking Judy's breath away and she was struggling to keep up with him. "Please," she gasped. "I've been trying to reach Dave – that's my husband – since he left for work, but he's not answering his phone and he didn't show up for the meeting he was supposed to go to. I'm terrified something's happened to him." The sympathy card was all Judy had left in her arsenal. "If something *has* happened, I'm not accusing you or blaming you, honestly I'm not. But I think you know *something* and I just want you to tell me. Please."

Edwin stopped abruptly and turned to face her. He looked silently into her eyes. Then he said,

"He doesn't love you, you know. Not like I do. You deserve so much better than him."

Judy could scarcely believe what she was hearing. "And that would be *you* would it?" she said, not even attempting to disguise her scorn. "What do you know about *me*, about *my* life? I'm very happily married and nothing *you* can say or do will ever change that."

The smile returned. "I fell in love with you the first time I heard your voice. I believe you felt the same thing." Edwin reached forward to touch her.

Judy swiftly stepped away from him. This was getting more surreal by the moment. "That's just ridiculous."

Edwin turned and started walking again. "Come on, the view from the cliff is magnificent."

Judy followed him. "Wait, you can't mean that silly incident at the pub?"

Edwin chuckled. "No. *Before* that. Think."

Judy frowned and shook her head. "Honestly, I have no idea what you're going on about."

"You called me."

Judy looked indignant. "I did no such…"

"You *called* me," Edwin repeated with a grin. He saw the look of confusion on her face. "Dear, sweet Judy. I can't believe I have to remind you." He looked at her lovingly. "Last week. Tuesday to be precise. Don't you remember? You asked me for a lift home."

Judy's mind was racing. "Wha…?" Then the penny dropped. "Oh, no, you've *got* to be kidding!" she exclaimed incredulously. "That *stupid* phone call? That was a misdialled number. You *know* it was. It was just a mistake."

They were nearing the cliff edge. Edwin stopped and turned to face Judy again. "But that's the point, it *wasn't* a stupid call. Don't you see? It was fate." He took a step towards her. Judy suddenly lurched forward and pushed him. "I've had enough of this… this… this claptrap!" she spluttered angrily, advancing towards him.

A look of surprise on his face, Edwin took a few paces back. She'd taken him off guard. Until now he'd held the upper hand, but suddenly this wasn't going the way he'd planned. "I can be everything you've ever wanted. Just come with me, let me show you. Please."

"Can you hear yourself?!"

"*Please!*" he repeated, his crystal blue eyes imploring her.

As he held out his hands to try to take hers, Judy's face filled with loathing and she lurched forwards again, forcefully pushing him away. "You're *fucking* crazy!"

Edwin's whole demeanour suddenly changed. This wasn't right; the Judy he loved would never speak to him like that. "But… But I *love* you."

"Love? This isn't love. It's some kind of sick, twisted *obsession!*" Judy was in full flow now.

She continued to advance on Edwin as he backed away from her. "You come to my shop, you come to *my* home, you terrorise me, you've done God knows what to my husband! And if you think I'm leaving here before you've told me, you're very much mistaken! What the hell's the matter with you? Honestly, this just isn't normal behaviour."

Edwin was almost lost for words at the vitriol she was hurling at him. What was wrong with her? All he'd done was declare his love for her. "But…"

Judy wasn't about to give him the opportunity to interrupt her. "Who the *hell* do you think you are? What gives you the right to treat someone like this? You should be locked up! *Love*?" She laughed sarcastically. "*Really*?!"

Edwin's face was etched with hurt – the same look Judy had seen the day he walked out of the shop. He hadn't realised that he had backed right up to the very edge of the cliff. But Judy had. Her eyes widened and she reached out an arm, but as she opened her mouth to warn him, the clump of grass on which Edwin was standing broke away from beneath him. In an instant he dropped vertically downwards, like a marionette whose puppeteer had taken a pair of shears to its strings.

Judy rushed to the edge of the cliff and dropped to her knees, peering over the edge.

As he'd felt himself slide, Edwin's hands had flown out and by pure chance he'd managed to grasp hold of a large piece of outgrowing root. There he hung, his face filled with horror, staring up at Judy. "Help me. *Please*."

Judy leaned forward as far as she dared and reached out over the edge of the precepice. "Quickly. Give me your hand." She shuffled forwards a few inches on her knees and as she did so another large chunk of earth beneath her hand dislodged. For one heartstopping moment Judy thought she was going to go over the edge, but she maintained her balance and the clod struck Edwin on the shoulder, then bounced off and continued its journey to the bottom of the cliff face. She moved forwards again and stretched out her arm as far as she could towards Edwin. Even as she did so, it occurred to her that even if she could reach him his weight might take her over the edge too. But she had to try.

Edwin looked up at her gratefully and carefully let go of the roots with his left hand. But his hands were wet from the rain and he felt himself start to slip. He kicked his feet against the cliff face to get purchase, loosening a sprinkling of mud and shingle. Looking up helplessly, beyond Judy's outstretched arm he could just see part of her panic-stricken face streaked with wet hair and mud. Even like that she looked beautiful, he thought and suddenly felt himself embraced by an all-consuming sensation of calmness and acceptance. He stared at Judy adoringly, his blue eyes sparkling. "I love you."

The thick piece of root supporting Edwin suddenly cracked and separated from the clump. With a howl of surprise he plummeted down the side of the cliff to the rocks below.

Gasping for breath, Judy dizzily rolled away from the cliff edge and lay on her back gazing up at the dark clouds, blinking as the needles of cold rain peppered her face. After a few moments, she sat up and put a hand to her head. Hearing a cry, she half turned to see Beryl, waving frantically, hurrying up the slope.

As Judy got shakily to her feet, Beryl reached her and threw her arms around her. "Oh my God, what happened?" she managed to wheeze. She stepped back and stared at Judy, her eyes searching for an explanation. "One moment he was standing right there in front of you, the next... he was gone!"

Judy shook her head. "I have to get away from here now."

"But..."

It was taking all the willpower Judy could muster not to burst into tears. "Please. We need to go. I'll tell you everything in the car. And I need to call the police."

Beryl nodded, put her arm around Judy's shoulders and guided her away from the cliff edge and down towards the car park. As they walked, Beryl craned her neck and looked back through the lashing rain in the direction of the cliff edge. There were seagulls beginning to circle and they were making the most infernal din.

On the rocks at the bottom of the cliff, Edwin's body lay motionless, mouth open, the vacant eyes staring skyward. One mangled leg had practically divorced itself from his body and his skull had been cleaved, depositing bone and brain matter across the white chalk.

A seagull landed beside him. It fearlessly hopped up and pecked curiously at his face. Deciding there was nothing here worth investigating further, with a beat of its wings it took flight and disappeared away into the horizon.

POSTSCRIPT

Dave had been lucky. Left with a severely twisted knee that he was warned would probably give him gip for the rest of his life – particularly during the winter time – he didn't *feel* particularly lucky. But that's what the consultant at the hospital had told him and, of course, when he later saw the state of his written-off 4x4, he'd realised the woman was right.

He had woken in a hospital bed to the pounding beat of music – "I was made for loving you, baby, you were made for loving me..." – and as he took in his surroundings he'd realised the sound wasn't coming from the room, it was pulsing in his head. He'd had no clear recollection of what had happened, but a nurse explained to him that some time after he'd spun off the road a passing delivery van driver had spotted the overturned car and immediately called for an ambulance.

Due to a nasty cut on the top of his head, he'd spent a night in hospital – purely for observational purposes. Then the next day a tearful Judy had arrived with Chris and Beryl to bring him home.

When the events of that fated afternoon on the clifftop revisited Judy – and they did so often over the weeks that followed, occasionally in her waking conscious, but all too frequently in nightmares – she would be left pondering whether, if she'd said or done something else, things might have played out differently. Dave had assured her time and again that there was nothing she could have done to change the outcome, and what had happened hadn't been her fault; Edwin had been a mentally unstable man and from what they subsequently learned from the police it seemed he'd been on an unwitting path of self-destruction for some while. Investigating officers had spoken to his employer in Rye and it transpired he'd been behaving out of character for several days prior to his visit to Eastbourne; further enquiries had revealed that it was likely he'd suffered some sort of an emotional breakdown, the culmination of what had apparently been a lonely, embittered life ruled by a cold and domineering mother.

Learning all this had changed nothing for Judy. Although she knew deep down they were all right, it didn't stop her thinking about what had occurred; that curse of the insecure, the compulsion to replay a past misfortune in your head, fully aware that it can't be changed, yet allowing the frustration to eat you up alive anyway.

Then one night several months later she had a lucid dream in which she found herself back on that deserted beach in France with her father. It was sunny and warm and they were sat together on the sand at surf's edge looking out across the sparkling water. "I miss you, Dad. So much." Her father put a comforting arm around her and as she snuggled into the crook of his arm – as she had done so often when she was a little girl – a powerful sense of safety and wellbeing consumed her. "There are things in life over which one has no control, my darling," he told her. "Bad things happen sometimes, but it doesn't mean they're your fault. And you're certainly not responsible for what other people do." He smiled down at her. How she missed seeing that smile. "You'll never be prepared for everything that life will throw at you," he told her. "You just have to do the best you can. Strive hard to defeat your insecurities and banish your dark dog days. And never, *never* let the self-serving behaviour of others make you question yourself." Her eyes brimming with tears, Judy gazed up into her father's smiling face. Planting a soft kiss on her forehead, he told her that he loved her and that he was proud of her. "And now, my darling, it's time to move on."

Judy woke up. After that she never dreamt about Edwin Colthorpe again.

The authors would like to thank:
Judith Ashford for the inspiration
Julie Elam for her support and encouragement
Sue Hards and Sara Greaves for proofreading

Front Cover Photo: Sara Greaves /
Edited by Rebecca Xibalba
Back Cover Photo: Rebecca Xibalba

Printed in Great Britain
by Amazon